D1525719

PANDEMICA

A SOUVENIR
OF A MOST DREADFUL YEAR

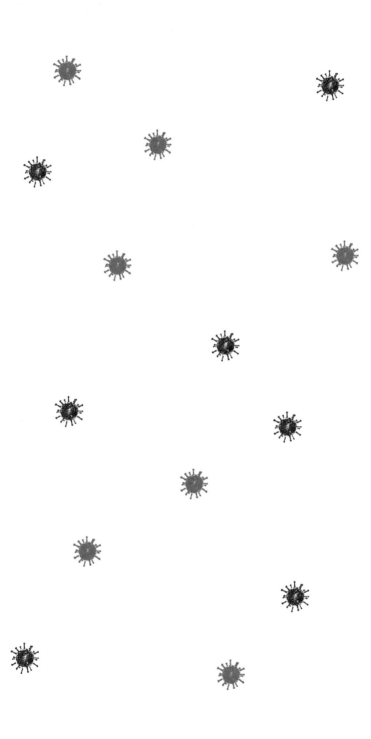

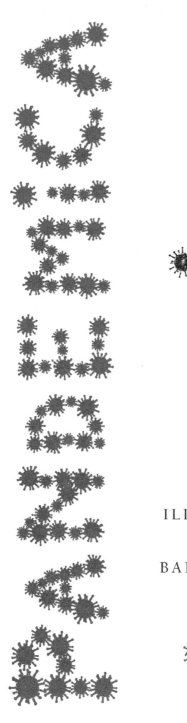
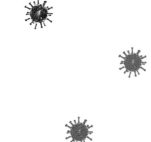

STORIES
AND
ILLUSTRATIONS
BY
BARUŠKA LIPSKI

#savethepoodles

PANDEMICA
A Souvenir of a Most Dreadful Year
Written and illustrated by Baruška Lipski

ISBN: 9798406274989

ACKNOWLEDGEMENTS

*My thanks to Carolyn Lengel for proofreading.
Since I made additional changes later on, and at times
went rogue with punctuation, any errors—whether
intentional or not—are mine, not Carolyn's.*

*Thank you to Carla Rae Johnson for organizing
the project "The Arc of the Viral Universe"
for which these stories were written.*

*I thank Tom Koken for his unflagging support
and keen eye, and Nancy Patterson for catching
a whole bunch more typos. It takes a village.*

*Special thanks to Gene Panczenko,
for his cheerleading.*

O human race, born to fly upward, wherefore at a little wind dost thou so fall?

—DANTE ALIGHIERI, THE DIVINE COMEDY

Fantasy is a necessary ingredient in living, it's a way of looking at life through the wrong end of a telescope.

—DR. SEUSS

We have it totally under control.
It's one person coming in from China and we have it under control.
It's going to be just fine.

—THE 45TH PRESIDENT OF THE UNITED STATES, JAN. 22ND, 2020

CONTENTS

INTRODUCTION

round mid-March of 2020, when grocery stores established special early morning shopping hours for old people (the most vulnerable population), I availed myself of the opportunity, since I have the dubious honor of qualifying for this privilege.

I'll never forget that first time I forced myself to go to Stop & Shop at the ungodly hour of 6:30 am. It was an alarming sight, and grim; all these sad, scared elderly folks wearing the pandemic uniform of sweat pants and face masks, silently shuffling past the nearly-empty shelves in search of the staples that we had always taken for granted, adding to their carts whatever they could grab before it was gone. It looked like a scene from a particularly dreary dystopian movie. Toilet paper being the holy grail, each elderly shopper would pause to look wistfully at the entirely depleted paper goods aisle, perhaps holding out hope that a truckload of Charmin would arrive just in time.

For our self-isolation entertainment, like everyone else who hadn't already seen it, my husband and I streamed "Contagion." I'd been warned that, on the brink of a real world pandemic, it would be too scary to watch. But it didn't really scare me much.

SPOILER ALERT!

It's just not scary when the epidemiologist who gets sick and dies is actually Kate Winslet. How many real epidemiologists look like Kate Winslet, anyway? Why can't casting agents give regular, human-looking actors these roles? I found her to be completely unconvincing in the part, being all cranky and serious and pretending she's not gorgeous. The scenes in that movie that did frighten me were the ones in which people behaved like animals, clawing at each other over toilet paper and snacks, since I could totally see that happening.

Anyway, faced with this dreary new reality we were living—no more eating out, or going to movies, or seeing friends, or travel—most people channeled their anxiety and boredom into baking sourdough bread. I channeled mine into making up stories.

P.S. The year 2020 already feels like a very distant past—just a ghastly nightmare from long, long ago, which makes these little fever dreams of mine now seem extremely dated, especially since almost everything I wrote was soon eclipsed by real-life events much crazier than I had the imagination to divine. It's been impossible to compete! So I think of these stories as small tokens from a weird year—a Cracker Jack box full of souvenirs that will soon be lost and forgotten: viruses, QAnon, super-spreader events, toilet paper hoarding, face masks, insurrectionists, campaigns, debates, Proud Boys, conspiracy theories, Oath Keepers, and the inescapable, depressing, exhausting, exhausting, appalling, infuriating, ubiquitous presence of the 45th President of the United States and his whole loathsome family. As far as presidents go, I hope it will never get any worse. But nothing, absolutely *nothing*, surprises me anymore.

FABRICATION

team of highly skilled computer scientists, designers, and engineers has been assembled, tasked with creating an automatonic replica of the Supreme Leader, Donald J. Trump.

The reason for the "decoy," as it's called, is that, in the unlikely event the Supreme Leader should contract and succumb to the virus in spite of his phenomenally robust health, his demise will be kept secret from the citizens, and the decoy used to create the illusion of continuous leadership. The purpose of this stratagem was to prevent further panic waves throughout the stock market.

The Decoy Design Team has been working diligently on the fabrication of the exterior. They've stretched burnt umber Naugahyde over the wire frame, to duplicate the Supreme Leader's outer epidermal layer (stratum corneum), aka "skin."

The team has found replication of the exact hue of his glassy blue eyes to be challenging, until their discovery that the preserved eyes of a lake sturgeon works perfectly. The Supreme Leader's lips have been fashioned from the anus of a baboon, and his hands from a toddler mannequin. A cocker spaniel pelt has been affixed to the top of the figure, completing the decoy's exterior.

The Artificial Intelligence Team has worked on recreating the exact degree of the Supreme Leader's intelligence. Since the team is accustomed to programming highly sophisticated systems, this task proved frustrating and demoralizing. In spite of this, they have accomplished their task with admirable professionalism.

The Engineering Team has utilized technology invented by Mattel, by means of which pre-recorded quotes from the Supreme Leader play when a string at the back of the neck is pulled and released.

The phrases include the following:

"We're winning. Like never before. Believe me."

"I call it the 'Fake News Media.' I invented the word 'fake,' you know. It's a terrific word."

"I am the best president of the last 500 years."

"It's a witch hunt."

"What is this disgusting green thing on my hamberder? Some kind of leaf? Who put it there? You're fired."

"The Art of the Deal is available wherever classy book-type things are sold."

"No collusion."
"No collusion."
"No collusion."
"No collusion."
"No collusion."
"No collusion."
"No collusion."
"No collusion."
"No collusion."
"No collusion."
"No collusion."
"No collusion."
"No collusion."
"No collusion."
"No collusion."

THE #1 SUPER-DUPER BEST SELLER

TRUMP

THE ART OF THE DEAL

FROM THE SUPER SUCCESSFUL STAR OF THE MEGAHIT TV SHOW

BY THE FUTURE SUPREME LEADER OF THE UNITED STATES

FLOTUS

The pandemic raged on. As the number of cases mounted, and the hospitals were overwhelmed, and the deceased piled up in morgues, and millions of Americans lost their jobs, Melania Trump became deeply distraught.

"Donald, it's terrible! Just terrible!" she cried to the Supreme Leader.

"Don't worry about it, Melanie. It'll all blow over soon, and I'll be re-elected. You'll still be First Lady. It'll be a landslide. We'll win bigly. You'll see."

"No, Donald, is not that. The hospitals, the doctor offices, they are full of sick people and I can't get my face tweaked! What to do? I see three new wrinkles, at least! My eyes, they are unsquinting! My face has slid down at least half inch! I want to be best! I'm scared, Donald!"

"Relax, Melody. I'm the Supreme Leader. I can get your face lifted. For free. Probably. Maybe."

"Donald, don't call it that. People will know."

He replied, "Okay, let's call it a 'kidney condition.'"

"Donald, no—we called it sick kidney last time. We need something new."

The Supreme Leader opened his laptop and scrolled through WebMD.

"How about cancer of the pussy?"

"NO Donald, I don't want them to think I have sick pussy."

"Brain tumor? Cirrhosis? Gallstones?"

"NO Donald! I don't want them to think I'm alcoholic or sick in brain. Gallstones are gross. I don't want them to think I have gross thing in me like that."

He kept scrolling. "Malaria?"

"Yes, Donald?"

"No, I'm asking you—how about malaria?"

"No, people get confused already; Melania, Malaria…keep looking, keep looking."

His attention span quickly fading, he said, "I could put Lindsey on this. Want me to?"

"Okay, Donald, ask Lindsey, if he make promise to not tell."

The Supreme Leader called his friend, Senator Lindsey Graham, and asked him for the favor.

"Linno, can you come up with some illness for Magdalena, so she can get her face lifted without people knowing?"

"Your housekeeper is getting a face lift?" asked a surprised Senator Graham.

"No, not her—the other one—the one I'm married to."

"Ohhhh…." said Graham. "You mean Melania."

"Whatever. Can you just come up with something terrific? Something very strong, but not too serious. Nothing too gross, though."

A short while later, Graham called back. "I got it! Malaria! They treat it with hydroxychloroquine! Great publicity for your drug!"

"She already said no to that. She's being tough, very tough."

"Well, then how about tonsillitis? We can say she's having her tonsils taken out."

"Tonsillitis. I like it. Young people get it, right? It will make her seem younger. It's sexy. Okay, tonsillitis it is. I think she'll go for that."

And so, a ward was cleared out at Inova Fairfax Hospital, one of the highest ranking hospitals in the nation. The Covid-19 patients were wheeled into tents in the parking lot. The First Lady's face re-tightening procedure was performed by a top plastic surgeon sworn to secrecy under threat of losing both his job and license.

After her "tonsil surgery," Melania's face was nearly touching her hairline, and her signature squint was fully restored.

"Thank you my darling! I could never leave you, no matter how desperately I want to!"

Her husband looked into the gleaming pair of coin slots that were her eyes, and said, "I like this face of yours, Melinda. It looks terrific. Just fantastic. The best face."

DREAM THREE

GOOBOOTWIT

As the pandemic dragged on, the number of people working remotely, socializing via Zoom, and shopping online soared, and the big tech companies seized the opportunity to lobby for deregulation. These were glory days for Big Tech.

Amid relaxed antitrust regulations, Google, Facebook, and Twitter merged to become GooBooTwit. GBT prevailed in defeating the Consumer Privacy Act. The Association of National Advertisers rejoiced, and GooBooTwit now has full power to collect users' personal data in one consolidated cyber data bank conglomerate.

Amazon rejoiced when Consumer Product Safety Commission approved their drones, in spite of serious technical issues. They are now in the air, everywhere you look, crashing into trees, birds, telephone poles, and each other. Drones are falling from the skies like so many miniature comets, landing in Walmart parking lots, backyard swimming pools, and school playgrounds.

Recently, in the skies above Palm Beach, two drones—one containing a 24-pack of toilet paper, the other, an industrial-size jug of hand sanitizer—collided head-on. Upon impact, the sanitizer caused the toilet paper to burst into a fireball, which fell and landed atop the head of the Supreme Leader himself, who was lunching on a triple-bacon-cheeseburger at his Trump International Golf Club.

OWWW!

The Supreme Leader was immediately rushed to the hospital by ambulance. Though they hadn't actually examined him yet, the excited and jubilant ER staff pronounced him dead on arrival. But when he suddenly bolted upright on the gurney and screamed, "OWWW!" the disappointed doctors and nurses got to work.

The fire had caused Supreme Leader's hair-like substance to melt and adhere to his scalp, so the medics ran his head under cold water, and, once it was cool enough to handle, loosened the hardened goo with turpentine and removed it with a putty knife. After carefully peeling off any remaining residue, they applied an antibiotic ointment to his damaged scalp. Despite some redness and blistering, the Supreme Leader was remarkably intact, thanks to a diet rich in preservatives.

Of course, the Supreme Leader did not appear in public until his replacement hair had been manufactured and re-attached. But attempts to keep the incident under wraps were foiled when it was leaked to the press, at which point the Supreme Leader tweeted, "More FAKE NEWS from the Lame Stream Media! I'm in perfect health and will NEVER DIE. But nice try, Losers!"

NOTE: Trump has reportedly played golf 308 times while in office, at an estimated cost to taxpayers of $145 million.

DUHH

 t's day 58 of the COVID-19 pandemic. Somewhere on the Upper East Side of Manhattan, a youngish gentleman in a bespoke cashmere suit sidles up to an unmarked door, and taps it three times. An eye appears at the peephole, and a voice asks, "What's the password?"

"Я ИДИОТ" the young fellow replies. The door opens and the gentleman quickly slides inside.

Within the velvet-lined walls of the room are banquettes, chaise lounges, a bar, and an enormous crystal chandelier. In an adjoining room are a stripper's pole, a jacuzzi, and a chocolate fountain. Behind a curtain is a self-serve Botox parlor. It is here that a mischievous group of coronavirus-skeptics who find it edgy, naughty, and exciting to defy the urgent warnings of epidemiologists have been gathering for regular soirees.

Calling their club "Dissenters United Happy Hour" (DUHH), the group's founder and host is none other than the perpetually tan, exceedingly vain, eternally randy sexagenarian and convicted felon, Roger Stone.

Among the better-known members of the club are Rand Paul, Rudy Giuliani, Caitlyn Jenner, Jim Bakker, Charlie Sheen, Jerry Falwell Jr., Tila Tequila, Wayne Newton, Gov. Ron DeSantis, Sheldon Adelson, Milo Yiannopoulos, Kristie Alley, and the My Pillow guy.

Newton and Jenner flirt by the bar. Giuliani and Falwell eagerly lick the edges of the chocolate fountain. Let's listen in on some of the conversations.

"Welcome, welcome, my friend! I certainly hope you didn't wash your hands!" chuckles Stone, as he greets the newcomer, shakes his hand, then glides his tongue across the man's palm. (This is DUHH's secret handshake.)

"Of course not!" laughs the young man, then licks Stone's hand in return.

Ms. Tequila purrs to Mike Lindell, "Have you been a naughty Pillow Guy?"

"Yes, yes I have! I haven't washed my hands in days!"

"Oooh, bad, BAD Pillow Guy!"

"I've been SO naughty! I used my pillow factory to make thousands of face masks that I had promised to donate, but instead I piled them up and BURNED them! Hee hee hee!!! PUNISH ME! PUNISH ME!"

"Oopsies! One of my false eyelashes fell into my cocktail," chortles Ms. Jenner.

"Let me fish it out for you," replies Mr. Newton, plunging his fingers into Caitlyn's drink, then sucking the champagne off of it before handing it back to her.

"How chivalrous of you! Let me clean off your fingers, sweetheart," replies Ms. Jenner, then licks each one.

Back in the Botox Parlor, Stone stands in front of a mirror and injects his face repeatedly.

"Isn't it time you made a speech, Darling?" asks Mrs. Stone. "You can get back to this right afterward."

"You're right, dear—I won't keep our guests waiting any longer."

Stone clinks his brandy snifter with a spoon. Ting ting ting!

"May I please have your attention! Let us raise a glass to that cunning little minx, the coronavirus! With her dainty ruby crowns, she deserves a name more befitting her regal power and beauty than one so dispassionate, so…*clinical*…as Novel COVID-19. Henceforth, we shall call her 'Queen Covidia Nouveau'! To those terribly unpleasant doctors and epidemiologists who want us to spurn our beloved Queen, hear this! You CANNOT take away our civil liberties! Nothing, NOTHING, will keep us from our God-given right to carouse, mingle, rub elbows (and other body parts), or lick any doorknob or light switch we choose to. Furthermore…."

Here the Rev. Bakker interrupts. "The End Times are upon us! We are on the verge of entering the Rapture! I'll be reunited with my darling Tammy Faye, and have four-ways for eternity with Tammy, Lori, and Jessica! YAHOO! PRAISE THE LORD!"

The room fills with shouts of "HEAR, HEAR!" and AMEN!"

"If only Roy Cohn could have been here," sighs Stone.

LET US RAISE A GLASS TO THAT
CUNNING LITTLE MINX,
THE CORONAVIRUS!

PERFECT

onald, look, says here many Democrats agree with you!" The First Lady was squinting hard at her iPhone. "Finally!"

"Huh?" asked the Supreme Leader.

"Yes, says here, 'He's right about one thing. If he stood in middle of Fifth Avenue and shoot people he would not lose votes.' Is true, you think, Donald? If you kill people, they like you still?"

"I don't know. Maybe. Probably. The important thing is that some Democrats finally agree with me on something. That's what you call bipartisanship."

"Try, Donald. Let's see."

So the Supreme Leader and First Lady hopped aboard Air Force One and within hours were in New York City, standing in the middle of Fifth Avenue. The Leader grabbed a SIG Sauer P229 double-action pistol from the holster of the nearest secret service agent, took aim at some tourists, and fired a round. Shocked screams filled the air, and people fell to the ground, gushing blood. Others fled in horror.

A stunned media responded swiftly.

"I'm shocked! Absolutely shocked! Unbelievable! Who knew that our Supreme Leader was such a superb, highly skilled marksman?!" marveled Sean Hannity.

"Just astonishing!" fawned Jeanine Pirro. "Well, he sure did show the American people what he's made of. He's unafraid.

He's strong. He's bold. He's everything you want in a strong, bold, unafraid leader."

Laura Ingraham swooned, "Wow. Just wow. And they thought Theodore Roosevelt was some kind of big brave he-man for shooting teddy bears!"

Democrats were less impressed. They demanded another impeachment trial.

Lindsey Graham, however, steadfastly disagreed. He angrily sputtered, "The Supreme Leader just did what most of us guys dream of doing, but are too afraid to do it. All the attention being heaped on this trivial, silly little thing is merely a tactic on the part of the Democrats to distract the American people from the Supreme Leader's many impressive accomplishments. They should be utterly ashamed of themselves!"

Capitalizing on the moment, the Supreme Leader immediately held a press conference.

"Why did you do it, Mr. Supreme Leader? WHY?" asked one reporter.

"Why did I do what?"

"Gun down your own citizens."

"I didn't. NEXT."

"Mr. Supreme Leader, it was recorded. We all saw it."

"That's not a nice question. NEXT!" He pointed. "You."

"To follow up on...."

"Who asked you? You're Fake News. NEXT!"

"You did. Mr. Supreme Leader. What was your motivation?"

"I'll tell you. It was a beautiful thing to see Democrats finally admit I was right about something. We're all in agreement. I brought our country together. It was perfect. And it was a perfect shot. Just perfect. But leave it to the Lamestream Fake News Media to make it into a negative. If Obama had done

28

the same thing you'd all be saying he's the greatest thing since sliced bread. What's so great about sliced bread, anyway? I can think of a lot of things that are much better than sliced bread. Sliced steak, for instance. Sliced Trump steak... it's beautiful, a beautiful thing. But it doesn't matter, because the people loved it. The American people. They loved it."

"So you DID do it!"

"I didn't say that. You said that. Next!"

Later, back in the White House, the FLOTUS jumped up and down and clapped her hands. "Oh Donald, that was big success! What fun! They love you! Do another! Do worse thing! More terrible even!"

"More terrible than shooting people? Stronger, that is? Like negative but in a positive way? But positively negative?

"Yes!"

"Like what? What could top that?"

"Make poop on White House lawn!"

"I'd love to, Melanie, but I can't. I can't. I just can't do that."

Thanks to a diet devoid of any speck of fiber, the Supreme Leader suffered from chronic constipation. He hadn't had a bowel movement in months—perhaps years.

"You still have pooping trouble, Donald? I give you something, make you poop. Old Slovenian remedy. Works like charm." She boiled radish seeds and cabbage in beet juice with some psyllium husks.

"I'm not going to drink that!" he said.

"You drink and I give you cheeseburger and ice cream, kind you like with cookie doughs mixed in. Maybe even blowjob."

He gulped it down.

Almost immediately he felt a roiling in his gut. He picked up the phone. "Kayleigh, quick—call a press conference right now."

"I can have one ready in forty-five…."

"NOW!!!" he screamed.

"YES SIR!"

By the time he'd run down all the steps and through all the hallways and reached the White House lawn—shoving secret service agents out of the way—the press was assembled. Sweating, clammy, red in the face, and unable to hold back one more second, he hastily pulled down his pants and squatted. Out oozed a steaming, fetid, noxious, dump, piled high in a thick swirl that ended in a delicate, upturned wisp, like soft-serve ice cream.

A stunned media responded swiftly.

"I'm shocked! Absolutely shocked! Who knew that our Supreme Leader was such a superb, highly skilled craftsman of excrement?" marveled Sean Hannity.

"Just astonishing!" fawned Jeanine Pirro. "Well, he did it again. He showed us he's unafraid. He's strong. He's bold. He's everything you want in a strong, bold, unafraid leader."

Laura Ingraham swooned, "Oh, my! Our Supreme Leader is not just courageous, but he's also unafraid to be vulnerable and show his sensitive side—his creativity. It just oozes right out of him! He truly showed America what he's made of."

Eric Trump proudly declared, "My dad is number one when it comes to doing number two!"

The Supreme Leader himself tweeted, "It was perfect. A beautiful, perfect bowel movement. The most perfectly formed bowel movement by anyone ever. Like no one's seen before. Everyone's saying."

HE'S EVERYTHING YOU WANT
IN A STRONG, BOLD,
UNAFRAID LEADER.

WAFFLES

Presidential candidate Joe Biden is about to give a speech. On his way to the podium, he stops to sniff a reporter's hair, but his handlers quickly pull him back six feet from the alarmed woman. He enters the plexiglass enclosure that encases the podium, and taps on the mic. There's a squeal of feedback.

"Is this doowacky on? Can ya hear me?" The feedback subsides, and he continues.

"OK. So, I heard today that our dunderheaded president has declared himself 'Supreme Leader for Life,' to be succeeded by Ivanka, then Junior, then that other guy, the real pale fella, and then Barron. Well, I say FIDDLESTICKS! This gibberish coming out of his butthole—which looks way too similar to his lips to tell which end he's talkin' out of, though there's really not much difference, if ya ask me—is pure MALARKEY!

"Mark my words—that snollygoster's so-called reign will end on January 20th, 2021! He's done nothing but flub the dub since he sat his fat behind down on his 'throne.' Until we can get rid of that nincompoop, we'll just have to pangle-wangle along as best we can.

"Now to my big announcement. This is gonna knock your socks off. Some folks had suggested I pick a gal as my running mate. To tell you the truth, it hadn't occurred to me, but once I got that bee in my bonnet, I thought to myself, 'Well, Joe, why the heck not? These days gals are doing all the same kinds of

SOME FOLKS HAD SUGGESTED I PICK
A GAL AS MY RUNNING MATE.

jobs that fellas do.'

"So, first I asked Oprah Winfrey. Folks seem to be quite taken with her—I hear she's real popular. And that would've helped me out with the lady vote and the African American vote, plus the voters who prefer TV people to us political types. Sadly, she turned me down, since she's real busy fixin' to put some of those book clubs of hers up on the World Wide Web.

"So I asked the closest thing to Oprah I could think of— Miss Gayle King. Well, Gayle jumped on it like a tick on a ground squirrel, and I'm over the moon about it!

"I just know that Gayle and I will make a really neat team, and I'll betcha dollars to donuts that she and Jill will become bosom pals.

"So, you're gonna start seein' a lot of yard signs and bumper stickers sayin' 'BIDEN-KING.' Which is kinda opposite of my wacka-doodle opponent's signs, 'KING TRUMP,' heh heh.

"Anyhoo, folks, the time has come for us to roll up our shirt-sleeves, put our noses to the grindstone, grease our elbows, shake a leg, take the bull by the horns, buckle up, knuckle down, get packin' and get crackin', zip up our trousers, lace our skates, butter our biscuits, gribble our grobbles, fiddle our faddles, and wiffle our waffles. And if we do our jobs right, we're gonna have one heckuva wing-ding come November fourth!

"Thank you, and LET'S MAKE AMERICA SWELL AGAIN!"

W T F

n a community center in Laverne, Oklahoma, Wendell Trevor Farnstock announces, "I hereby call this meetin' to order!"

Wendell and his twin brother, William Taylor Farnstock, known jointly to their friends and followers simply as "WTF," are cofounders of the Coalition of Coronavirus Hoax Resisters and Freedom Fighters (CCHRFF). The members affectionately call themselves "Chrffers."

Wendell continues, "We're gathered here today, in a decidedly undistancey way, I might add…" (the crowd chuckles) "…to discuss this so-called pandemic."

Now William speaks up. "Everyone here knows this thing is a bunch of fake-news horse-shit, or else we wouldn't be here, right, Chrffers?"

There are shouts of "HELL, YEAH!"

Wendell says, "That's right, Will. It's a HOAX, cooked up by Soros, Buffet, Gates, and some of their other rich snowflake buddies. There's a virus goin' around, but it ain't no killer—it's just a regular ol' flu. Who here thinks we should shut the whole damn country down, put people out of work, keep 'em from their livelihoods, unable to feed their families, just 'cuz a few people got the sniffles?"

The room fills with voices yelling, "No way!" "Hell no!" A voice from the back shouts, "I got the sniffles now, but I ain't gonna quit my damn job over it!"

Wendell continues. "This whole scary boogeyman virus thing was made up to try 'n' bring the Supreme Leader down. Why? Because those guys HATE him. Why? Because he's richer than all of 'em put together, AND because they're jealous that he's married to a beautiful piece of ass, AND because he's a real true American patriot...he loves God and country and all the little unborn babies headed for abortions, and they just HATE him for it!"

The crowd murmurs and nods in agreement.

William adds, "Wendell's right. Furthermore, we learned from a reliable source, RealFuckinTrueConspiracies.com, that this virus, this coronavirus, it was cooked up in a laboratory in Wuhan, China, by a bunch of Oriental scientists. They looked for the two meanest, nastiest, ugliest, most ornery viruses they could find and stuck 'em together in a petri dish and mated 'em, and voila! The coronavirus was born. Then they squirted that sucker into a bunch of their own people and shipped those poor bastards over to our shores to infect America with it. Why? Because they want to make us weak so they can take us down, and turn America into a Communistic country and make us worship that fat little turd, Kim Jong Fong instead of Our Lord and Savior, Jesus Christ."

Wendell speaks again. "And it's quite possible that Soros, Buffet, Gates, and the like were in cahoots with the Chinese government to make this happen."

Someone yells, "AND Obama!"

"Yep, prob'ly him too. Why? To get a bunch of American people dead and fuck up our economy and try and make the Supreme Leader look bad and incompetent and real stupid."

An elderly farmer in the front row stands up.

"Wait a minute there, WTF. First you say it's a hoax, just

made-up hooey. Then you say it's a real actual virus that was cooked up in a lab and brought over here. Which is it? It can't be both!" The room goes silent.

Wendell narrows his eyes and says, "Why can't it be?"

"It makes no sense!" replies the farmer. "Being fake and real at the same time. Is it a hoax? Or was it brought over here to kill us? It's gotta be one or t'other. Being both just ain't logical!"

The brothers glance at each other and sigh. Wendell squints up at the ceiling; Will looks down at the floor. Then, speaking very slowly, as if to a low-IQ child, he says, "I'll let you in on a little secret, my friend. There's no such thing as 'logic.' Logic is an elitist, libtard invention, concocted just to confuse people like you and me. They'll throw it in your face every damn time. 'Wah! Wah! It ain't logical! It ain't rational! Boo hoo! Boo hoo!'"

The crowd laughs. The farmer looks embarrassed.

Wendell adds, "Will's right. I googled it up, and it turns out it was invented by some li'l ol' Greek boy named Aristotle, who made up a bunch of gibberish about hypertheticals and syllogisms and quantum-whatevers. The libtards just eat that shit up and 'gurgitate it, thinking it makes them look smarter than you and me, because they're insecure little snowflakes, with long fakey words but not a lick of common sense. Don't fall for it! If you try to be logical back at 'em you'll only end up with a big ol' headache. Will here knows more about it than I do. Will?"

"Let me tell you the definition of logic." Will pulls a small dictionary out of his back pocket. "Ahem. 'Logic. Noun. Reasoning conducted or assessed according to strict principles of validity.' So, friends, just WHOSE principles of validity are the reasons being assessed by? Not yours! Not mine! Is that right? Is it fair?"

"No it ain't!" yells someone in the back. "It's a trick they pull to try to distract you from what you're pissed off about!"

"Yup," says Will. "Next time one of 'em tries to pull that 'logic' B.S. on ya, just yell a lot of insults at 'em. That usually shuts 'em up."

Wendell adds, "And it always helps to have a gun. Now let's everybody take a pee break and meet back here in twenty to discuss our next move. Help yourselves to coffee and cookies in the lobby."

Meanwhile, in a secret lab in Wuhan, scientists have been conducting experiments, injecting wasps with the DNA of scorpions, crocodiles, and black mambas. The result? The deadly Asian murder hornet, soon to be unleashed on an unprepared America.

TURNS OUT IT WAS INVENTED BY SOME
LI'L OL' GREEK BOY NAMED ARISTOTLE.

PANON

An anonymous, high-level government official who is privy to top-secret classified information and goes only by the letter "P" has been communicating in the form of code about a vast cabal of right-wing poodle-philes who traffic in sex with underage poodles. These people also produce poodle porn. Participants are purported to engage in perversions pertaining to poodle pee and poodle poo.

Just who IS "P"?

Some have pointed to "P" possibly being President Pootin, who professed to possess pictures of the POTUS (aka "PEETUS") playing in puddles of poodle piddle, having parlayed his passion for prostitute pee into a new and novel perversion. (When his penchant for poodle pee was leaked, PEETUS was pissed. He denied it very strongly, saying "Preposterous! I prefer pussy.")

Unlike PEETUS, Vice President Pence is a poodlephelia proponent, proclaiming the Bible prophesied the propagation of a population of poodle-people.

"It is Providence that people and poodles intermix. Besides, I prefer a pretty poodle pup, with those perky little puffs, to Mother Pence. I'm pleased and proud to partake in God's plan."

"P" claims the cabal reaches all the way to the upper echelons of government. He has reported on the prevalence of private parties where poodle pups are procured for the pleasure of Pentagon personnel.

"These poor pups are made to provocatively parade around

in panties while partygoers watch," reported "P." "Preposterous as it may seem, things can quickly progress from leg-humping and heavy petting to copulation, doggy-style."

"P" has warned that the poodle population is in profound peril. Proponents of "P" promote pursuing, prosecuting, and imprisoning all pimps who prostitute poodle pups.

OPERATION WARP SPEED

 t was a gray, rainy day. The Supreme Leader was sulking because he couldn't play golf. The First Lady said, "Donald, don't sulk. Can't you find other thing to do besides golfing, always golfing?"

"Other things? What other things?"

"You are Supreme Leader of United States. Is Monday. You have some presidenty things to do, no?"

"Work is for losers, Melanie. I have people to do the work for me. Lindsey. Pence. That skinny blond lady who looks like a piranha."

"Kellyanne? She needs boob job."

"Her husband's not very nice. I'm thinking of firing him."

"You cannot fire him, Donald. He does not work for you."

"Okay, I'll fire HER then. I've been meaning to anyway. She gives me the creeps. Her eyes don't match. Besides, if she was at all loyal to me, she would have divorced him by now." He sniffed. "I guess I'll go oversee the OWS guys."

"Huh? What is owls guys?"

"O.W.S. Operation Warp Speed. They're working on a Kung Flu vaccine. Really, really, fast. At warp speed! That was my idea! Do you like it?"

"Sure, Donald, brilliant as always," she said, rolling her eyes.

"I'm going over to the lab."

The Supreme Leader went down to the White House's basement bunker. He grabbed a Diet Coke from the mini fridge, then walked over to a framed portrait of himself on the wall. Behind the portrait was a gold keypad. He pressed 8 7 8 6 7 ("TRUMP") and a bookcase filled with copies of "The Art of the Deal" glided over to the right, revealing an elevator. He stepped inside and pressed a button. The door closed. Down, down, down the elevator went—for a very long time—during which he sipped his Coke and watched Fox News on a small screen.

It finally stopped on level X. The door slid open. Lindsey Graham was sitting in a golf cart parked next to the elevator door. The Supreme Leader hopped in next to Graham. The men looked at each other and flicked out their tongues, wagging them left to right in a secret greeting. Graham drove the cart silently down the hallway, and stopped in front of a heavy steel door marked "BOILER ROOM." The Supreme Leader hopped out and Graham drove off. The Leader pressed a button next to the door, and a female voice came through the intercom.

"Password."

"Man. Woman. TV. Camera. Uh…TV." He waited. Nothing happened. "God dammit, Evilyn, it's me, Donald! Let me in!" The door opened.

A striking raven-haired woman in a black leather corset and spike-heeled boots, holding a whip, purred, "Welcome to Operation Warp Speed, Mr. Supreme Leader. To what do we owe the pleasure of this visit?"

"It's too rainy to golf, so I thought I'd stop by and oversee things. And I think Melanie wanted me out of the house," he chuckled.

He looked around the lab. It was dank, and smelled of mildew. Against one cinder block wall, three starving, filthy epidemiologists were shackled and chained. The Supreme Leader had fired them from OWS because they'd insisted on conducting trial studies, which was certain to delay having a vaccine ready before Election Day. They were being kept in the lab so they couldn't talk critically about the Supreme Leader to the Fake News Media.

Barron Trump was spoon-feeding one of the three of them some porridge from a bucket.

"How's the summer job going, son?" Trump asked.

Barron shrugged. "Okay, I guess."

The epidemiologist spat out a mouthful of porridge and wailed, "You're going to get us ALL KILLED! Not just us, but ALL your citizens! These idiots you brought in to replace us— they know nothing about vaccines!"

As he spoke, the Supreme Leader moved his hands in and out as if playing air accordion. "You epidermatologists… so overrated. Who wants to study germs for a living? Only losers. Sad. Germs are disgusting. Anyway, I know more about

WELCOME TO OPERATION WARP SPEED,
MR. SUPREME LEADER.

epigerminology than anyone. So do these guys," he said, jabbing a thumb toward two men in white lab coats.

One of the men, Mike the My Pillow guy, was hunched over a Bunsen burner, while the other, Kid Rock, was injecting a mouse with a brownish solution.

"How's it going, guys? Will it be ready soon? The election is only a couple months away. Whatcha got there, Kid?"

"No worries, man, we got this. I'm squirtin' this little dude with a vaccine I made from Lysol, cranberry juice, Clorox bleach, and a little bit of Budweiser, to help it go down easy. There'll be a Bud Light vaccine for folks who are watching their waistline."

One of the epidemiologists cried out, "You don't guzzle a vaccine, you moron!"

Said another, "Please listen to us! A vaccine needs antigens to trigger the immune system to produce antibodies. Swigging beer, bleach, and Lysol will do nothing but get people killed!"

Mistress Evilyn cracked her whip against the floor and screamed, "SILENCE!!!"

"Don't listen to them, Kid—you're doing great, just great. But add some hydroxychloroquine to it. We acquired a crap-load of that stuff…we gotta use it up."

"Not one mouse has gotten sick yet, so it seems to be working. Some died, but I don't think from Covid," said Kid.

The epidemiologist in the middle fumed. "That means absolutely NOTHING! You need to do clinical trials with human subjects to demonstrate a vaccine's efficacy and safety!"

"I SAID SILENCE!!!" screamed Mistress Evilyn. "One more word out of you and you're getting a lit firecracker up the ass!"

Shooting the epidemiologist an angry look, Kid Rock continued. "AS I was saying, the next step is trying it out on human subjects." He gave a sidelong glance the direction of the shackled men.

"So these losers might be useful after all, eh?" chuckled the Supreme Leader. "Pillow guy! What are you up to?"

"I'm cooking a batch of Red Bull and meth, with a couple shots of espresso. It's for me and Kid, so we can go at this vaccine at warp speed."

"Very good, very good. Warp speed!" the Supreme Leader said, smiling and moving his clenched hands as if steering a race car. "Terrific work, guys. We'll have a perfect, beautiful vaccine, just in time for my re-election." He turned to the epidemiologists. "We'll show you losers and that Fauci guy how it's done. Barron, give them some water. I want them to live just long enough to witness my yuge victory."

Barron dipped a sponge into a pail of water, then held it up to each of the prisoners' mouths. "Dad, if I can't have a puppy, can I keep one of these guys?" he asked.

"No pets, son. You know that."

"But, Dad, I'll feed and water him and...."

"NO PETS!!!" screamed Evilyn, cracking her whip.

"Jeez, Evilyn, you can't talk to my son that way! You're fired!"

He winked at her and mouthed "not really."

"Sure, son—you can keep just one, as a pet. I'll have Lindsey build a cage. But your mother's gonna kill me...heh heh!"

The Supreme Leader glanced at his watch, and said, "Whoops. Gotta get going—it's almost time for Hannity."

COVID CAN'T TOUCH ME
BECAUSE I AM COVERED IN
THE BLOOD OF CHRIST!

DREAM TEN

THE BLOOD OF CHRIST

To say no to President Trump would be saying no to God.*

If God tells you to give $12.99, do it. Whatever the Holy Spirit speaks to you. If you need to give by credit card, do so.*

—*Paula White, chair of Donald Trump's Evangelical Advisory Board*

he following is an infomercial by Paula White, chair of the evangelical advisory board in Donald Trump's administration.

"COVID CAN'T TOUCH ME BECAUSE I AM COVERED IN THE BLOOD OF CHRIST! And now, YOU can be, too!

"Let me explain.

"The Lord recently sent me a vision. Nancy Pelosi, Chuck Schumer, George Soros, Hillary Clinton, Bill Gates, Mitt Romney (you heard me right... Mitt's gone over to the dark side), and SATAN HIMSELF were dancing hand-in-hand (butt naked!) 'round a circle of fire, cackling their demonic cackles as flames licked up skyward, and the sulphur smell of Satan's sweaty armpits mingled with the noxious fumes of this vile, unholy coven of heathens. They danced faster and faster, and screeched louder and screechier, 'til they finally collapsed in a sweaty, stinky heap. That's when the orgying started up—all of 'em suckin' and slurpin' on each others' private areas in a mad frenzy, including homosexually, since there were only two girls to four guys.

"Once they were all tuckered out, they lit up cigarettes and started discussing the plague they were plotting to use to bring down our beautiful, blessed country.

"Gates came up with the plan to shoot coronaviruses out the tops of cell phone towers, and make them radiate out of people's TVs and microwaves...and believe me, he has the know-how to do it.

"But then all of a sudden a miracle happened! God blessed me with the power to save his faithful by bestowething upon me full, unfettered access to the blood of His only son, Jesus Christ! And He instructed me to find a way to shareth it with YOU, my devoted flock.

"Does Matthew 27:25, 'May his blood be upon us and upon our children' ring any bells? Well, it ought to! And by golly now you CAN have His blood upon you AND your entire family, with our His Most Precious Blood® line of products!

"Don't be fooled by imitations! Only OUR Blood of Christ is certified genuine 100% Jesusblood, bottled at the source. It's available in 1.5 liter bottles and in 6-packs of 12 oz. cans, perfect for church suppers and big family gatherings. We also have convenient JB Power Packets®—just add water and stir—as well as Save Me Savior® lozenges, for when you're on the go!

"I tell you, His Most Precious Blood® is SO versatile! Not only will it protect you from most viruses, but it can be used in many different ways. Anoint your scalp with His Most Precious Blood® to banish dandruff to the gates of hell. Smooth it around your eyes to correct unsightly dark circles and crow's feet. Or simply pour it over your head for a full physical innocculation and spiritual edification. Used in suppository form it will deliver you from constipation and soften those hard stools that I call 'Satan's briquettes.'

"I'll betcha you're thinking, 'Sounds awesome, Paula! But real blood of Christ must be CRAZY expensive!' Not with our subscription plan, it isn't! Your customized orders will be delivered FREE, for a monthly donation of just $91! Now I'll bet you're thinking, 'Well, that's a funny number, Paula! Why $91?' I'll tell ya! It's because Psalm 91 says, 'He is the one who will rescue you from hunters' traps and from DEADLY PLAGUES. Makes sense? And now, let us pray.

"May God's holy spirit enter and speaketh through me RIGHT THIS VERY MINUTE in His mysterious and heavenly language! Eno derdnuh srallod ro erom lliw eetnaraug uoy a ecalp ni nevaeh…etirw ruoy skcehc tuo ot aluaP etihW siert-siniM thgir won! And may His Most Precious Blood®, which flowed from the wounds of our Lord Jesus cleanse us and protect us from all viral-type sicknesses. And one more thing, dear Lord; please watch over and protect and bless your most perfect creation, the Supreme Leader Donald J. Trump. Amen."

Real, true quotes from Paula White.

MID-BOOK COCKTAIL HOUR

Now that you're approximately half-way through this book, how about a cocktail break? Have the pandemic blues wiped out your liquor cabinet? Afraid to venture out to the liquor mart? Being sober is a little too, well, sobering in these challenging times. No booze? No problem! Fall back off the wagon with these delicious semi-alcoholic beverages!

- COOL MINT JULEP
  In a tall glass, muddle some parsley with Crest Clean Mint tooth paste. Fill with Cool Mint Listerine and ice. Garnish with a stick of Wrigley's Spearmint gum.

- "GIN" FIZZ
  Fill glass with Pine-Sol, drop in two Alka Seltzer tablets, top off with a spritz of PAM cooking spray.

- DAYQUIL SUNRISE
  Dissolve one packet of Cherry Kool-Aid and one packet of Tang in a highball glass filled halfway with water. Top it off with orange-flavored DayQuil and ice. Garnish with a cherry cough drop.

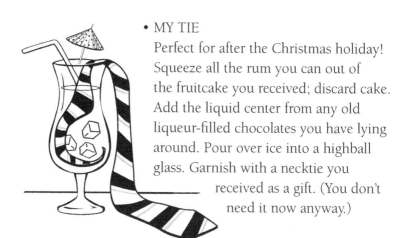

- MY TIE

  Perfect for after the Christmas holiday!
  Squeeze all the rum you can out of
  the fruitcake you received; discard cake.
  Add the liquid center from any old
  liqueur-filled chocolates you have lying
  around. Pour over ice into a highball
  glass. Garnish with a necktie you
  received as a gift. (You don't
  need it now anyway.)

- MUCINEX MULE

  Combine windshield wiper fluid and as many bottles
  of vanilla extract as you can find in your cupboard
  into a chilled tin can filled with ice. Garnish with a
  Mucinex DM lozenge.

- WINDEX SOUR

  Combine equal parts Windex and
  Mountain Dew into a cocktail shaker,
  and shake vigorously. Pour into an
  old-fashioned glass filled with ice.
  Garnish with a Sour Patch Kid.

IMPORTANT DISCLAIMER:
DO NOT, UNDER ANY CIRCUMSTANCES, MAKE OR CONSUME THESE DRINKS!

I CAN'T TWEET

The Supreme Leader's steadfast supporters gathered all across the country in a National Day of Resistance to march in protest of Twitter having flagged falsehoods he had tweeted, like when he claimed he had proof that Chinese take-out restaurants had been cooking Covid-19 viruses into their egg rolls and duck sauce.

In another tweet he warned, "With voting by mail, you get thousands and thousands of Mexican illegals hired by Dems to fraudulently sign Fake Ballots SO WRONG!!! Plus mail boxes will be robbed and ballots.....

.....will be forged and signed by child Sex Slaves chained up in Crooked Hillary's basement, the SAME illegal kids who are taking Good Jobs away from American sex workers UNFAIR!"

But when he tweeted that his genitalia was much larger than those of his predecessor, "...really tremendous, and more beautiful, quite frankly, that's what they're saying..." it was one lie too many, and Twitter banished him permanently.

A National Day of Resistance was quickly organized in response. All across the country, protesters showed up at rallies with muzzles over their mouths to symbolize their leader having been censored. To make sure their muzzles were not mistaken for coronavirus masks, they had the words "This ain't about no virus! MAGA!" embroidered on them. Some marchers wore masks with a hole punched out at the mouth, so they could smoke.

As they marched, they chanted, "I CAN'T TWEET! I CAN'T TWEET!" When one marcher was asked by a journalist if the similarity of this chant to the one regarding police violence inflicted on people of color was perhaps insensitive, he replied, "To our Supreme Leader, tweeting IS breathing! Suffocating our Leader's free speech is a helluva lot worse than what those brave law enforcers did to a couple of bad apples!"

Another marcher piped up, "Correct me if I'm wrong, but last I heard, this is a free country! Twitter is violating our leader's God-given right to make up whatever bullshit he wants to! Hell, birds are still allowed to tweet, but not the Supreme Leader of the United States! Goddamn birds have more civil rights than HE does!!!" With that, he blasted his M85 into the sky, and several sparrows, some robins, and a woodpecker fell to the ground. "If our Supreme Leader can't tweet, neither can YOU ASSHOLES!" he screamed at the dead birds. The crowd of marchers cheered and started shooting rounds of ammo at every bird they saw.

When the Supreme Leader learned of this show of support, he grabbed his phone and typed, "Some very Fine Patriots stood up very strongly today to some terrible avian thugs.....

......it's no wonder bird numbers are going down, birds are overrated LOSERS that shouldn't be allowed to migrate from shithole countries to ours. Our wall must be built much higher and IT WILL! MAGA!"

But when he tried to tweet it out, it wouldn't go.

SWANS SONG

Ahistoric meeting of the Strategic World Assembly of Non-human Species, aka SWANS, is taking place. SWANS is made up of a consortium of representatives from nearly every nonhuman species on the planet.

The Secretary-General of SWANS, a polyphemus moth, taps the mic with his antenna, then speaks.

"My fellow nonhuman residents of our beloved planet, it appears that we are beginning to shake off the invasive species known as humans. We still have a long road ahead of us, but much progress has been made toward their decline, thanks to the diligent efforts of many. First and foremost, we want to express our gratitude to Mother Nature for her innovative creation, COVID-19. Mother, would you please stand and take a bow?"

An enormous womanly form rises up from the ground. She is adorned in worm silk, wildflowers, and moss. Her hair—a tangle of switchgrass, leaves, and vines—flows down past the knobby roots of her feet. Bees and butterflies swirl about her head. She waves her tree-branch arms gracefully in the breezes that perpetually surround her, and blows kisses. Pollen sprinkles from her rosebud lips. Applause in the way of slapping fins, clomping hooves, and beating wings fills the air. She continues blowing kisses as she slowly recedes back into the earth.

The Secretary-General continues. "We give our heartfelt

A POLYPHEMUS MOTH TAPS THE MIC
WITH HIS ANTENNA, THEN SPEAKS.

thanks to all the species that have gone before us in trying to mitigate this existential threat—the pigs who carried the swine and Spanish flus, our crustacean friends who helped spread cholera, the mosquitos who armed themselves with Zika, the tireless camels for distributing MERS, and the heroic horseshoe bats who doled out SARS. Today, we recognize those brave pangolins who made the ultimate sacrifice for the cause."

More applause, along with some whistles, bleats, and trills.

"Thus far, those valiant efforts have been insufficient to quash our powerful foe. Today, our mission is more urgent than ever. If we don't eradicate the human species for good, we are facing certain doom, as is our Mother." The moth chokes back a sob. "I'll now pass the mic to the chair of the Polar Bear Partnership."

The polar bear speaks up. "The ice floes we call home are rapidly melting. The polar bear diaspora will continue unless things change very soon, if it's not already too late."

Next to speak is the Ambassador of The Marine Life League. "The oceans are still a mess," says the narwhal. "However, there's been much less trash, sewage, and oil being dumped into our home since the cruise ships stopped operating. It's imperative we keep up the momentum, lest these deadly cruises resume."

A monarch butterfly lands on the mic. "As representative of the International Insect Alliance, I gotta tell you, we're in trouble. Speaking for myself and all my monarch sisters, after migrating 3,000 miles, we're beat—we need a soft place to land. But we can barely find any milkweed anymore! And we're supposed to lay 300 to 500 eggs along the way? Pfff...get real!"

The boss of the Rodent Syndicate grabs the mic. "Whoa whoa whoa...wait just a minute. Us rats depend on the humans for food. It's been mayhem in the 'hood since the garbage disappeared. We've been forced from our sewers out onto the streets in broad daylight to look for some chow. It's humiliatin,' but we're starvin'! I ain't had no pizza in weeks! Quit picking on the humans; they've been real good to us." His comments are met with hissing from the snakes and geese.

The Secretary-General again speaks. "As I said, we have a ways to go, but I think this time might be different. The human race is devolving. Thanks to recent sharp increases in human stupidity and selfishness, we may just have a fighting chance at survival, especially because of some exciting news which I'm about to share.

"The permafrost is melting, so ancient viruses and bacteria that have been preserved in frozen soil for thousands of years are now springing back to life, fresh as a daisy! It looks to be a mishmosh of viruses and microbes, anthrax and tetanus spores, even botulism! A whole 'Pandora's box' of pathogens. To talk a little more about this, here's Pandora." He hands the mic to the renowned Greek damsel.

"Hi, there. So, the permafrost is like this big ol' box I used to have, the one I never shoulda opened because a whole buncha the worst crap imaginable came flying out of it, and then everybody blamed ME for unleashing all the evil and suffering in the world. Yea, me and Eve...we women always take the blame for all the bad stuff that happens because we supposedly beguile men with our..." (here she makes air quotes) "...bewitching beauty and seductive charm...blah blah blah. Gimme a break—like it's OUR fault for being irresistible instead of THEIRS for being so pathetically unable to keep their pollinators in their pants! Anyhoo, right before I closed the box, out flutters this one tiny, adorable sprite named Elpis, also known as 'Hope.' SO, my point is that the permafrost is like my box, see? Along with all the gross, disgusting stuff that's gonna be released, there will also be a tiny glimmer of hope—the hope that these pathogens will wipe out that entire race of douche bags once and for all. To be perfectly honest, I don't know whether or not that includes me, since I'm a person, but also a myth. Whatevs. Either way, I'm willing to make the sacrifice, for all of you, and for our Ma Earth." She hands the mic back to the moth, who looks a bit taken aback.

"Thank you, Pandora. Ahem. Moving forward, our assembly's Permafrost Task Force is currently researching ways to utilize this important opportunity to its fullest potential. It's still in the development stage, but so far the studies have been very promising. And now...."

Several more speeches by various creatures ensue, after which the moth returns to the stand to say, "I thank you all for attending. In closing, we have a few words from our chaplain."

A praying mantis climbs up to a jack-in-the-pulpit. "Thank you, Mr. Secretary-General. Ahem.

"I do believe the day will come when we shall see our beloved planet begin to heal from the terrible ravages inflicted upon us by our oppressors. And when that day comes, joy and jubilation will ring out throughout the land, skies, and seas, from the highest mountaintops to the deepest depth of the ocean." Here his voice rises in both pitch and power: "And ALL Earth's creatures, every fern and every flounder, every sparrow and every slug, from the mightiest sequoia to the most humble flea will join wing, fin, and tentacle and sing, in the words of the old Blackbird spiritual, FREE AT LAST! FREE AT LAST! THANK GAIA ALMIGHTY, WE'RE FREE AT LAST!"

A tremendous roar fills the air.

AND ALL EARTH'S CREATURES WILL JOIN
WING, FIN, AND TENTACLE AND SING,
IN THE WORDS OF THE OLD BLACKBIRD
SPIRITUAL, FREE AT LAST! FREE AT LAST!
THANK GAIA ALMIGHTY, WE'RE FREE AT LAST!

SPACE FORCE

n the day that the COVID-19 pandemic reached its zenith, the Supreme Leader stood in the middle of Launch Pad 39B at the Kennedy Space Center to deliver an address.

"Today I stand on this historic launch pad, where many wonderful astronauts have launched, to talk to you, the American people, about the newest branch of our great military, the U.S. Space Force, which, by the way, was my idea.

"First of all, I'm announcing my decision to replace Space Force Chief of Staff, Gen. Charles Q. Brown, with myself. I'm the best choice to run the Space Force, because no one knows more about space than I do. I know a lot about space, believe me. I've been around space my whole life. More than perhaps anybody. I don't know, maybe. Maybe. So I hereby name myself to be Supreme Commander of Space Force. I'm the first American President in history to be both Supreme Leader and Commander of Space Force at the same time. No one else has done that. Just me.

"As Commander, I have made some other changes to the top leadership. Secretary Barrett, Chief of Space Operations Raymond, and Chief Master Sergeant Towberman have been replaced by Ivanka, Don Junior, and Barron. Some in the Fake News Media have questioned the qualifications of these replacements. I assure you these candidates were personally vetted by me, and are perfect—couldn't be more perfect.

"The USSF Secretary should be someone with a really terrific figure who looks good in the Secretary's uniform, which I chose myself; a low-cut silver mini-tunic and thigh-high boots. I considered Melania for the position—she'd be terrific—but, quite frankly, Ivanka is much more qualified.

"So, what is the purpose of Space Force? Our mission is to boldly go where no man has gone before. Obama didn't go there, no one else has gone there, George Bush didn't go, neither did George Junior or low-energy Jeb. Only I can get us up there. To space.

"Our top priority is to seek and find Crooked Hillary's 30,000 emails. They're floating around somewhere up there in cyberspace. Space Force will find and retrieve them. Believe me.

"Another goal is to protect and defend our planet from coronaviruses and the other alien invaders that want to destroy our way of life. Obama made our military very weak, almost broke. It's now bigger and stronger than ever, thanks to me. I've invested fifteen billion dollars for procurement of a fleet of beautiful new Hummer military spaceships, each one carrying an arsenal of powerful weapons for defeating our enemies: turbolasers, interplanetary ballistic missiles, super-sonic light-sabers, space grenades, and proton torpedoes. And we will have material for even more powerful weapons, once we defeat Pluto and take their Plutonium.

"Also, we will claim ALL of outer space for our great nation! All those stars and planets, all those beautiful stars—aren't they so beautiful? And the planets, they're just tremendous. And they're all going to be ours, the United States of America. We will plant our beautiful American flag on every star and planet.

"After we've secured all the stars and planets, we will get busy building luxury Trump hotel-and-casinos, timeshare properties, and Trump Interplanetary Golf Clubs, all over the galaxy. By the way, we're offering special deals for qualifying earthlings on flexible club memberships to any of our beautiful, prestigious, classy Trump vacation timeshares. For details, go to: www.WhiteHouse.gov/timeshares.

"More good news! I have reacquired the Miss Universe Pageant! We will finally have contestants that truly are from all over the universe—some green ones, some blue ones, some with three boobs—it'll be fantastic.

"Last but not least, we are going to build a wall around our planet. Some very bad space aliens are coming to Earth from other galaxies. When they send their extraterrestrials, they're not sending their best. They're bringing space germs. They're bringing bedbugs. They want to anally probe our women. Some, I assume, are good aliens.

"For instance, Gort, leader of Mars, is very good, very tough. I read on RealTrueConspiracies.com that Gort abducted and probed Joe Biden, so he may have some inside information. GORT, IF YOU'RE LISTENING, IF YOU HAVE ANY DIRT ON SLEEPY JOE, CALL ME.

"But the other aliens, the ones that aren't so nice—like the ones from Uranus, they're some bad actors. You know they call it 'Uranus' because it's a shithole planet, and shit comes out of Uranus. YOUR anus, not mine. I don't shit; haven't in years. It's a disgusting habit, I would never do something like that, believe me.

"And finally, a special surprise! To commemorate this historic day, I assigned my son Eric to go on USSF's very first manned mission. Eric will be the first person in history to be launched into space on the beautiful new StarTrump Galaxy® Jetpack. It's still in the development stage—this one's a prototype.

WE WILL FINALLY HAVE CONTESTANTS WHO
TRULY ARE FROM ALL OVER THE UNIVERSE—
SOME GREEN ONES, SOME BLUE ONES,
SOME WITH THREE BOOBS—
IT'LL BE FANTASTIC.

However it's been looking very promising, very promising. We'll see how it goes with Eric.

"Besides testing the StarTrump Galaxy® Jetpack to find out if it works, Eric's mission is to collect space dust and moon rocks, explore black holes, and zap any coronaviruses he comes across.

"Eric, are you ready? TAKE OFF THAT HELMET—IT MAKES YOU LOOK WEAK!"

Eric removed his helmet (a launch engineer rushed over and put it back on), buckled his seat belt, then gave his father a big grin and a thumbs-up. A voice from the control tower began the countdown.

"Ten seconds to liftoff....

Nine,
eight,
seven,
six,
five,
four,
three,
two,
ignition..."

ERIC WILL BE THE FIRST PERSON IN HISTORY
TO BE LAUNCHED INTO SPACE
ON THE BEAUTIFUL NEW
STARTRUMP® GALAXY JETPACK.

DEBATE NIGHT!

artha Raddatz is moderating the first presidential debate. The candidates are a good distance apart, behind plexiglass barriers. Martha opens with the following question:

RADDATZ: President Trump, you're 74 years old, and Vice President Biden, you're 77. Some Americans are worried that both of you are too old to handle this highly complex job. How do you respond to them?

BIDEN: Thank you, Martha. I'd say this to the American people. With age comes experience. Heck, I have more experience than a Galápagos turtle's great-great grandpa! And wisdom up the wazoo! Why, you could fill a great big huckleberry basket with all the wisdom I've accumulated over the years.

TRUMP: Sleepy Joe doesn't have wisdom. I'm the one with wisdom. And brains. I have the best brain. The best brain. Person. Woman. Man. Camera. TV. Let's see YOU do that, Joe.

BIDEN: No problem. Person. Woman. Man. Camera. TV. Now watch this! TV. Camera. Man. Woman. Person. See? I just did it backwards! Can you? Well? Can you?

TRUMP: Yes, and much faster, too. The Apprentice. Camera. Me. Pussy. Me.

BIDEN: You want backwards? I'll give ya backwards. VT. Aremac. Nam. Namow. Nosrep. Top that!"

TRUMP: Lindsey, get me some stairs.
(Graham rushes over and places a short set of steps in front of him—the kind people provide for their elderly pets. He helps Trump to the top step. Breathing heavily, Trump descends the five stairs, pausing on each one.)

Person. (pant)
    Ivanka. (pant)
        Hannity. (pant)
            Camera. (pant pant)
                Fake news. (pant)

(Clutches his chest.)
When I did this for the test, the doctors, they couldn't believe it. They'd never seen anything like it before. No one's ever done it. Only I can do that.

BIDEN: (Leaps forward into a handstand.)
Person. Gal. Fella. Camera. Boob tube. How about THAT? Your turn. Go.

RADDATZ: Let's move onto the next question. President Trump, some say your response to the coronavirus epidemic was sluggish and that many deaths might have been prevented if a plan had been implemented earlier. Why wasn't the federal government better prepared to deal with this emergency?"

TRUMP: Person. Woman. Me. Camera. TV. See? I did it again.

RADDATZ: Yes, I see. Could you please address your slow response to the pandemic?

TRUMP: That's such a nasty question. I had the fastest response to any pandemic ever. You know it. I know it. First, I made it so the Chinese couldn't fly over here to spread their Egg Flu Young. Next I ordered everyone to wear masks. The masks were my idea. No one wanted to wear them until they saw me wearing one. All of a sudden everyone wants to wear masks! They saw how good I look in mine. Now everyone's wearing them, thanks to me. People can't get enough of them. Masks. It's unbelievable. Person. Woman. Man. Camera. TV.

BIDEN: C'mon, man! That's pure MALARKEY and you know it! You never put on a mask until it was painfully obvious to the American people that you were being arrogant, stubborn, and just plain IGNORANT by refusing to wear one!

TRUMP: (Quickly places a mask on his face.)
Oh? Where's your mask Joe? I have mine on. Where's yours?

BIDEN: Why the heck are you wearing one NOW? You don't have to wear a mask for this debate! Can you believe this circus pony rodeo clown?

TRUMP: (Quickly removes his.)
What mask? I'm not wearing a mask. Martha, do you see a mask on my face? Sleepy Joe is clearly senile and deranged. Sad!

I MADE IT SO THE CHINESE
COULDN'T FLY OVER HERE TO SPREAD
THEIR EGG FLU YOUNG.

RADDATZ: Let's just skip to your closing statements. Mr. Vice President, please go first.

BIDEN: Thank you, Martha, and thank you Amazon, Anheuser-Busch, and Pizza Hut for sponsoring this debate. As many love to point out—heh heh—I've been around a while. So I've seen our great nation go through its ups and downs. But never, EVER could I have imagined I'd see the day when my country would be so torn apart and divided as it is today, or be putting young children in cages, or be devastated by a plague that threatens both our lives and our livelihoods—one that could have been avoided with sound leadership. Our great nation has lost her standing in the world. Other countries aren't just laughing at us—they PITY us! If you're ready to TRULY make America great again, join me. Please go to www.joebiden.com. God bless you, and God bless the United States of America."

RADDATZ: President Trump—your closing statement?"

TRUMP: I'm the best president since Lincoln, that's what they're saying—some say maybe even better. Obama never thought of masks. I did. Keep America great! No collusion. Person. Boobs. Jared. Thing. TV."

C'MON, MAN!

I'M A PET AND I VOTE!

AND MANY WERE SENT TO DEAD PEOPLE AND MANY WERE SENT TO—A NUMBER WAS SENT—I GUESS, TWO—THAT AT LEAST TWO, THREE, FOUR WERE SENT TO DOGS. ONE WAS SENT TO A CAT.*

—*True quote by the President of the United States, August 13, 2020*

After hearing that ballots had been sent to dogs and cats, the Supreme Leader's worries over voter fraud were keeping him up every night.

"This is very, very bad," he said. "Mail-in ballots are being sent to pets. Those pets aren't supposed to be voting. They don't have the right to vote, so it's illegal for them to be voting. And ballots, they're coming in from other countries. They say some ballots are from pets that weren't even born here.... German shepherds, Irish setters, Mexican Chihuahuas, Shih Tzus from China, Afghan hounds—some of them are with the Taliban. This is a very, bad situation. Very bad."

The Supreme Leader decided to recruit a coalition of volunteers to investigate any mail-in ballots that looked suspicious, in order to guarantee a completely fair landslide victory for himself. So he dog-whistled to Bikers for Trump. At first there was no response, because he'd used an actual dog whistle, which the bikers couldn't hear. So he followed up with another, more audible announcement.

"We're looking for some really tough, strong people to look

for fake ballots, that aren't real ballots. Or, as I call them, 'fake ballots.'"

Soon an eager group of Bikers for Trump was assembled, and Operation Landslide Victory was launched. Their first task was to sort through millions of mail-in ballots and pull any that had suspiciously pet-like names.

"Jesus! Here's one from a 'Mittens Goldstein'! C'mon... who are they kiddin'?" exclaimed one volunteer.

Other ballots were pulled, with names like Fido Esposito, Towser Finegold, Fluffy Manzino, Smokey Ohlmeyer, Socks Brinkley, Shadow Horton....

Three of the bikers—Wayne, Ron, and Duke—were among the first to be dispatched to investigate a ballot. They rode their Harleys 335 miles from the nation's capital to 212 Crestview Drive in Franklin Park, PA. After parking in the driveway of a modest ranch house, they rang the doorbell. A kind-looking elderly woman answered.

"Why, what a surprise! Are you Judy's grandsons? She said she'd send her grandson over to help me with my TV. I certainly didn't expect three of you!"

"Where's your cat?" demanded Wayne.

"Boys, I don't have a cat."

"Your dog then."

"I'm sorry, but I don't have a dog either. I don't have any pets. I'd love to have one, but, at my age, they're just so much trouble to take care of. Mr. Goldstein and I used to have a little bichon frise named Princess. Oh, she was just the cutest little fluffball! She used to...."

"We're looking for Mittens Goldstein. Mittens tried to vote, which is illegal."

"What?! Since when is it illegal to vote?"

"Cats can't vote, lady! It's illegal!"

"Like I told you, there are no cats here. I'M Mittens Goldstein. I've been voting since 1948. I voted for Dwight Eisenhower and I haven't missed a single election since then. In fact, I already mailed in my ballot. I'm voting for Joe Biden. The Republican party isn't what it used to be. I'm almost glad that Mr. Goldstein isn't alive to see what's become of...."

Fuming, Ron said "YOU'RE A LIAR! NO HUMAN BEING IS NAMED 'MITTENS'! BRING US YOUR CAT! HE'S UNDER ARREST FOR VOTER FRAUD!"

Mittens Goldstein looked stunned. "Since when is it illegal to have an unusual name? Look at all those Palin kids, up there in Alaska! They have silly names like Twig, and Stick, and Trout...."

"Those aren't cat names. 'Mittens' is a cat name," said Duke.

"And what's YOUR name?" she asked Duke, squinting at the the embroidered name on his jacket.

Duke shuffled his feet. "I'M asking the questions here, lady. Why the hell is your name 'Mittens,' anyway?"

"That's a wonderful story. After I was born, my parents had an awfully hard time figuring out what to name me. They tried many different names, but none of them quite fit. They tried Boots, and Fluffy, and Midnight.... Then they noticed I had an unusual amount of hair on my hands for a baby, and...."

"Never mind," said Wayne. "We gotta get going."

With that, the bikers hopped back on their Harleys and took off to Moline, Illinois to investigate one Fluffernutter Johnson.

Meanwhile, a secret meeting was taking place in a location I'm not at liberty to disclose.

"I hereby call this meeting to order!" announced the chair,

Pickles McGowan. "Lucy Panczenko, please go first."

Said Lucy, "So, Black human men got the right to vote in 1870. White human women got the right to vote in 1920. By 1965, pretty much EVERY human had the right to vote. But here we are, in the year 2020, and dogs and cats STILL can't vote! It's not right!"

Loki Pierson chimed in. "We're Americans, too! The laws that affect this country affect us all! Why are puppy mills still legal? Why are homeless dogs and cats kept in prison camps? WHY AREN'T THERE MORE DOG PARKS???"

Sparky Girardi shouted, "Trump's afraid of the power of pets! He's trying to disenfranchise us because HE knows that WE know that he's an ASSHOLE who hates animals!" She paused to compose herself, then continued, "Let us now join paws and sing our anthem, 'Hold the Lantern High.'"

Pickles asked everyone to form a circle and join paws, except for Sparky, who gently waved her own tawny paw in the air as she led the group in song.

HOLD THE LANTERN HIGH

We are several million strong
And we know it won't be long
When every dog and cat will have been freed.
Our brothers and our sisters
With wet noses and dry whiskers
Shall come together and declare our creed.

(*chorus*) So hold that lantern high
There's no ceiling to the sky
Every pet a suffragette
The time is nigh!

With our humans by our side
We shall hold the lantern high
And signal that our time has finally come
Though you think that we're not smart
We have brains, and we have heart
Unlike the Supreme Leader, who's SO dumb!

(chorus) Now's the time to heed our cry
To hold that lantern high
Every pet a suffragette's
The flag we fly

Every cat and every cur
Let us bark and let us purr
Our voices ringing out in harmony
Pussycat and setter
Yes, our futures will be better
As we march in unity towards Galilee

(chorus) So hold that lantern high
And perhaps we'll have some pie
Suffragette for every pet
The time is nigh!

Yes, we'll hold the lantern high
There's no ceiling to the sky
Suffragette for every pet
Now let's have pie!

78

I'M A PET AND I (WANT TO) VOTE!

My Dearest Melanie,

I have rec'd your letter today. It gives me great pleasure to know that you and Barron are in good health. I'm sure the lad has grown fine and strong since last we were together. It hardly seems possible it was a mere fortnight ago that my brave army stormed the Capitol building, captured the podium, and then set up encampment inside the Rotunda.

Your ennui ...

Mrs. Melanie Trump
1600 Pennsylvania Avenue, NW
Washington, DC 20500

FORT ROTUNDA
JAN 6

FROM STATUARY HALL THEY SHALL
TURN TOWARD THE EAST UNTIL REACHING
MADAM PELOSI'S STRONGHOLD.

80

A Letter from the Commander in Chief of the Revolution to His Wife

My Dearest Melanie,

I have rec'd your letter today. It gives me great pleasure to know that you and Barron are in good health. I'm sure the lad has grown fine and strong since last we were together.

It hardly seems possible it was a mere fortnight ago that my brave army stormed the Capitol building, captured the lectern, and then set up encampment inside the Rotunda.

You enquired as to my condition. I am quite well, my darling. Despite the discomfort of our bunks, I am sleeping soundly. 'Tis apparent that the dissolution of my Twitter account has had a salutary effect on my health; I feel refreshed and rejuvenated with the vigor of a man half my age. Oh how I savor the sweet irony—the coward Jack Dorsey's foolish attempt to muzzle me has backfired bigly, as I now lay claim to full, restful nights of slumber, and am more robust than ever!

As I write this letter, I pause to gaze upon the majestic painting of the Founding Fathers signing the Declaration of Independence, displayed above my command post. It stirs my soul, and fills my heart with pride to honor these noble men by defending their glorious creation, these United States, against our mortal enemy, that treasonous woman, Nancy Pelosi. Or, as I call her, "Nancy."

Tomorrow, before dawn, the men in my command shall embark upon a long and treacherous journey. From our

Rotunda encampment they shall march northward to the Senate Chamber to capture the flag and plant in its place our magnificent MAGA flag. They shall then circle back south, through Statuary Hall, and march onward to the House Chamber. From there they shall turn toward the east until reaching Madam Pelosi's stronghold.

Once the troops arrive, their mission is to rifle through Madam Speaker's drawers, defecate on her chair, urinate on her carpet, expectorate into her pen-and-pencil cup, and masturbate into her potted plant. Pillaging office supplies shall be encouraged, as these writing implements, sticky notes, staplers, and other various desk accessories belong to WE THE PEOPLE, paid for with OUR hard-earned tax money.

The troops shall then begin the long trudge back to our encampment, perchance pausing at the gift shop along the way for souvenirs to commemorate this important day in history.

Alas, there is a high probability that I shall be unable to accompany my battalion. Though I wish more than anything to march alongside these brave men, I am suffering with the most terrible pain from my heel spurs, which, vexingly, are acting up again after lo these many years.

I shall be with them in spirit, however, and I have every confidence that these men will be ably led by my second-in-command, a loyal soldier of impeccable character, Field Officer Angelli. You have seen him on the news, and remarked upon his fetching fur headdress, intriguing Valknut tattoo, and his perfect nipples. Indeed, I dare say you may be more than a little smitten! (-;

Enclosed herein, my darling Malaria, you will find twenty-five dollars, which I liberated from Mike Pence's desk drawer. Put it toward the necessary renovation work to your face.

One more thing. It is most urgent that you send me another package as soon as you are able, as we are running dangerously low on both rations and supplies. We have been subsisting on nothing but hardtack and salt pork. Please send a generous number of Big Macs and Diet Cokes. Also, liquid bronzer. Astonishingly, there is nary a tanning bed in all the Capital Building. (Just what IS our tax money going to? Smh.)

I miss you terribly, my fair and gentle wife, and cannot wait to be reunited with you and young Barrett once again.

Pray for my safe return, my Darling.

xoxo

Love always,
Your Commander

VICTORY OVER PENCE DAY

— *Real true quotes from the 45th President of the United States* —

MONDAY, JAN. 4TH, 2021

"I HOPE MIKE PENCE COMES THROUGH FOR US, I HAVE TO TELL YOU.
OF COURSE, IF HE DOESN'T COME THROUGH, I WON'T LIKE HIM AS MUCH."

TUESDAY, JAN. 5TH, 2021

"THE VICE PRESIDENT HAS THE POWER TO REJECT
FRAUDULENTLY CHOSEN ELECTORS."

WEDNESDAY, JAN. 6TH, 2021

"IF MIKE PENCE DOES THE RIGHT THING WE WIN THE
ELECTION. ALL VICE-PRESIDENT PENCE HAS TO DO IS
SEND IT BACK TO THE STATES TO RECERTIFY AND WE
BECOME PRESIDENT AND YOU ARE THE HAPPIEST PEOPLE."

LATER THE SAME DAY....

"MIKE PENCE DIDN'T HAVE THE COURAGE TO DO WHAT
SHOULD HAVE BEEN DONE TO PROTECT OUR COUNTRY AND
OUR CONSTITUTION, GIVING STATES A CHANCE TO CERTIFY
CORRECTED SET OF FACTS, NOT THE FRAUDULENT OR
INACCURATE ONES WHICH THEY WERE ASKED TO
PREVIOUSLY CERTIFY. USA DEMANDS THE TRUTH!"

nside the Capitol, two mahogany boxes containing the Electoral College votes were placed before Vice President Mike Pence. He was to preside over the final step in certifying the election results. Ordinarily an uneventful formality, on this day tension was running high. Vice President Pence had made it clear that he refused to follow the Supreme Leader's orders to throw out the election results and hand him the victory. Outside at the White House Ellipse, an ever-growing crowd of fervent supporters gathered for the "Stop the Steal" rally. They excitedly waited for the Supreme Leader's speech.

But first let us go back a few months, to early October 7th, 2020, the day that Bartholomew Fleugon's life changed forever.

Bartholomew "Buzzy" Fleugon was a common housefly who had landed on the head of Vice President Mike Pence during the Vice Presidential debate. Buzzy was crawling around, minding his own business, completely oblivious to the fact that he was on national television, when he suddenly noticed the bright lights and camera, and froze. He remained that way on camera for a two full minutes and three seconds before snapping out of it and flying off to a window ledge to regain his composure.

But he didn't go far. In fact, little do people know (including Pence himself) that from that moment on, Buzzy rarely strayed from the Vice President. For he realized that, overnight, he'd become the most famous fly in the world! He was appearing in photos on the front page of newspapers. He was the darling of late-night TV talk shows. There were internet memes of him, and clever cartoons. Everybody loved him! It thrilled him to his core to know how much joy he'd brought into people's lives.

Buzzy also had to admit that he found that taste of fame

intoxicating, and craved more of the spotlight. Some accused him of having become a fame-whore, but Buzzy didn't care. For the first time ever, his life had meaning—a higher purpose than just breeding and spreading pathogens. He figured he owed it to his many fans to appear in public with Pence wherever and whenever he could. To that end, he stayed close to the Vice President, patiently awaiting his next chance to be on camera.

Sadly, though, after the debate, the public's interest in both the Vice President and Buzzy quickly faded.

However, Buzzy didn't mind just hanging out with the Vice President. You see, he'd grown quite fond of the man. He enjoyed crawling around Pence's hair, the color of freshly fallen snow. It was always immaculately groomed, and redolent with the fragrance of coconut, bergamot, and jojoba oils from his leave-in scalp conditioner.

When he wasn't hanging out on Mike's head, Buzzy would explore the Pence home at Number One Observatory Circle. He'd investigate the pantry and waste baskets, knock around inside lampshades, or sample what was left in the food dishes belonging to the family pets—Harley, Hazel, and Marlon.

Whenever Mike had a late-night dish of ice cream (they both loved strawberry) Buzzy would sneak some when Mike wasn't looking, but he preferred to pretend they were "sharing."

Buzzy's mortal enemy was the housekeeper, Josefina, who was forever chasing after him with a fly swatter, yelling "FUERA, MALVADA MOSCA!" But he was always too quick for her, and enjoyed taunting her by staying just out of reach.

The lifespan of a housefly is tragically short. But Buzzy was determined to beat the odds and hold out until at least January 6th, the day his friend would certify the election results. He told himself it was because he wanted to witness history, but deep down he knew the truth; it would be his last chance to appear on camera in front of the entire nation before Pence was to leave office.

The Big Day was finally here. He'd made it! Buzzy rode with the Vice President in his limo up Independence Avenue to the Capitol Building. Though he had been on this route many times before, this time Buzzy choked up a bit as the limo passed by the Lincoln Memorial, then the Washington Monument, and at last the Capitol reflecting pool before pulling up to the Capitol building's rear entrance. Once inside the Senate Chamber, Buzzy discreetly crawled down to the edge of Mike's hairline for a clear view, then sat back and rubbed his forelegs together while waiting for the proceedings to begin.

Outside at the rally, the Jumbotron screen finally filled with the Supreme Leader's orange visage. The crowd roared!

"This is a very special day in our country's history," he began. "Today is a day that will live on in infirmity. It's the day we take back our country from the losers and haters who tried to steal our beautiful country from us. I asked Traitor Mike to do one favor for me. One TINY favor." (The word "TINY" came out with his signature gurgle.) "And did he? Did he do it?"

"BOOOO!!!" shouted the protesters.

"Our election was rigged by the radical leftists—they rigged the election. They rigged it like they've never rigged anything before. You beautiful patriots, look at all of you—you're so beautiful. So much love. We're going to march down Pennsylvania Avenue. I'll be marching with you in spirit only, because of my heel spurs, but I'm still marching with you, believe me. Today we will make that history together. The best history. Because you know what we're going to do. What we have to do to save our democracy."

"HANG MIKE PENCE!!!" shouted the crowd.

While the Supreme Leader prattled on, an impatient group headed off to the Capitol building, with more and more people joining them along the way. "We're going in!" yelled one. "This is OUR house!" yelled another. All the while, the crowd continued to chant their rallying cry—"HANG MIKE PENCE! HANG MIKE PENCE!"

A little while later, there was a sudden commotion inside the Capitol Building, along with a sense of panic that Buzzy didn't understand. Capitol police were swiftly ushering legislators out of the chamber. The legislators seemed rattled. Buzzy was scared and confused. He sensed that the Vice President needed to leave too. Why was Mike dilly-dallying?

The Vice President had gone to his office and was carefully gathering up an armload of all he could carry, to take into lockdown—his framed family photos, his King James Bible, his lunch box, his pocket Book of Psalms, his "World's Best Vice President" mug, his New Living Bible....

A police officer appeared in the doorway.

"Mr. Vice President, you must come with us now," he said.

"The protesters—they've breached the building!"

"Just one sec—I'm looking for my American Standard Pocket Bible."

"Mr. Vice President, forget about these things—it's urgent that we go NOW!"

"Maybe it's in here…" muttered Pence, rummaging through a desk drawer.

"Now, Mr. Vice President. I mean it. NOW!"

But he'd dawdled too long. Insurrectionists were in the hallway, hooting and hollering. Mike peeked out to take a look. A big ruddy-faced man with a handlebar mustache spotted him and yelled, "Hey! There he is! THERE'S PENCE! GET HIM!!!"

The mob rushed at the Vice President. Buzzy flew over and tried to beat his wings against the mustache guy's eyeball, but a housefly is no match for a 295-pound male human, who just brushed him off.

A fellow named Wayne, who was wearing a paramilitary camo-print jumpsuit, goggles, and combat boots, grabbed the Vice President and held him in a chokehold, while another, Dwayne, sporting a gas mask and a big furry pelt with a bushy tail, sprayed Mike with pepper spray (Buzzy flew quickly out of the way). Then another guy, by the name of Zayne, yanked off the MAGA flag he'd been wearing as a cape and proceeded to tear it into long strips. Others joined in to help twist the strips into rope-like pieces, which Wayne, Dwayne, and Zayne used to tie up the Vice President's hands, knees, and feet.

Mike struggled helplessly as they carried him aloft out of the Senate Chamber and into the daylight. All the while, the rhythmic chanting of "HANG MIKE PENCE!" hung in the air like an ominous drumbeat.

The police officer who'd been trying to escort Pence to safety picked up the Vice President's cell phone, and called Karen.

"Mrs. Pence, I'm a Capitol Police officer. I'm sorry to have to tell you this, but the Senate Chamber has been breached by domestic terrorists and they've taken your husband. You should come right away. I don't know what they're going to do to him."

"Oh shoot, I can't right now," replied Karen. "Charlotte and I are getting mani-pedis. We'll come as soon as we can, I promise, once our nails are dry."

"Mrs. Pence, I believe the situation is very dire. Where are you? How soon can you get here?" He didn't have the heart to tell her what the mob had been chanting.

"We're at the Hair Today, Nails Tomorrow beauty salon—not far at all. We can be there in a jiffy, after our nails dry. I'm sure you policemen have everything under control."

Overhearing the conversation, Buzzy immediately left Mike's head and beelined it over to the Hair Today, Nails Tomorrow beauty salon, just three and a half blocks from the Capitol Building. He knew exactly where it was, since he had once been to the salon's dumpster to feast on birthday cake residue from some paper plates and candles.

He arrived at the salon to find Karen and Charlotte browsing magazines while their toenails were drying. Holding up a page for Karen to see, Charlotte said, "Mom, what do you think of this jumper? Do you think it would look good on me?"

Flying in frantic circles around the two women, Buzzy shouted, "Come quick! Mike's in trouble! Those crazy MAGA idiots mean business, for real!" But all the two women could hear was "Bzzzzzzzzt bzzzzzzzzzzzzzz."

"I'm not sure, Honey. Yellow's not your color. You're awfully sallow."

"How about this?" asked Charlotte.

Now hysterical, Buzzy screamed at Karen, "Mrs. Pence! Are your toenails really more important than your husband's life?" Then to Charlotte, "OR YOUR FATHER'S???"

"Oh, Honey—I love it! That would be just SO adorable on Audrey!"

"GO HELP MIKE! TALK TO THOSE PEOPLE! THEY'LL LISTEN TO YOU!!!" But all the women heard was "Bzzzzzz bzzzzzzzzzz bzzzt." Buzzy started dive-bombing first Karen, then Charlotte.

Flapping her hand at Buzzy, Charlotte said, "What's with this fly? So annoying!"

Buzzy landed on the tip of Charlotte's big toe and waved his front legs at her. "For the love of God, LISTEN TO ME!!!"

"Gross!" Charlotte said, before flicking him off her foot. Woozy from the chemical odor of still-tacky nail polish, Buzzy flew unsteadily to the counter and stumbled around, trying to get his bearings. Karen rolled up her magazine to give him a smack.

Back at the "Stop the Steal" rally, the Supreme Leader continued his speech. "Today we will make history together. So much history. Believe me. Incredible. Because you know what we're going to do. What we have to do to save our democracy."

The protesters shouted "HANG MIKE PENCE!!!"

"That's right, that's right, we're gonna hang Traitor Mike." Cheers filled the air.

"The Vice President had the power to fix it, but Traitor Mike wouldn't fix it. He wouldn't fix it. Because he's a traitor. Mike Pence was nobody until I came along and made him Vice President. No one even knew who he was. They said 'Who is this Pence? Who is this guy, Pence? Mike Pence? Never heard of him.' A nobody. I turned him into a Vice President. Nobody could do that but me. And did he thank me? Where were the thanks? Unbelievable. After all I've done for him. So unfair! Vice President. I did that. But couldn't even say the election was rigged. He could've stayed on as Vice President, instead he wants to be a loser. He said to me," (he affected a high-pitched, mincing voice) "'No, Sir, according to the Constitution I can't do this, I can't do that…I don't have that power, Sir, blah blah blah…' So guess what, Mike…guess what we do to cowards and traitors?" He held his hand around his own throat, rolled his eyes up comically, and lolled his tongue out. The crowd went wild.

At Hair Today, Nails Tomorrow, Buzzy began to come around. His thorax was partially collapsed—just enough to affect his equilibrium. He sat awhile, resting. Then he looked around for others of his species to help him, but there appeared to be none within the salon. He was alone. He tested his wings. At first he could only move one, pivoting it in slow circles, and buzzing. He stretched both wings akimbo, raising and lowering them—at first slowly, then faster and faster and faster—until they were fully flapping, and soon…. He was aloft! Due to his compromised equilibrium, his flight was a bit wobbly, but at least his wings were functioning normally. He returned to the National Mall surprisingly fast.

Bartholomew Fleugon arrived just in time to see his friend's body being carried aloft by Dwayne, Wayne, and Zayne toward a makeshift gallows. They rolled Mike onto the platform, then propped him up on a stool. Knowing that, as a mere fly, there was nothing he could do, Buzzy flew onto Mike's head, so he would at least be with his friend through this terrible ordeal, for whatever it was worth. He crawled down toward Mike's temple.

"Hey!" said Wayne. "Look! It's that fly!"

"What the hell are you talkin' about?" said Zayne.

"That fly that was on TV! It was on Pence's head during the debate! Remember?"

"YES, YES!!!" shrieked Buzzy. "IT'S ME!!! I've stayed with Mike this whole time! At the beginning, I admit, I was only in it for the fame, but as I've gotten to know him, I've come to love and respect him. You've got him all wrong! He cares deeply for his country—that's why he refused to throw the election! He loves God and family! His hair smells fantastic! Why are you doing this? Why? WHY???"

Dwayne asked, "What makes you think that's the same fly that was on TV? I mean, what are the chances?"

Wayne said, "Seriously, man, I recognize him! I know my flies. I have a Phd in entomology, with an emphasis on house-flies. I worked as a medical entomologist for the Air Force for eight years."

Dwayne looked at him suspiciously. "Are you one of those edjucated elites?"

"Used to be. I'm reformed. After my wife left me for another entomologist, one specializing in fireflies—I guess she found that more glamorous or exciting or sumthin'—I went into a tailspin. I started drinking, smoked weed, did coke, did meth, did oxy, did speedballs, lost my job, hit rock bottom, got sober, got saved, found God, found Jesus, found Fox, found Trump, found Parler, found Oath Keepers, found QAnon…and here I am!" He grinned. "Now I work for myself, running my own business, 'America First Pest Control.'"

"And so what if it IS the same fly? Let's get on with this, man! We're makin' history!"

"HE'S RIGHT! I'M FAMOUS!" screamed Buzzy! "DON'T

KILL MIKE! PLEASE! HE'S MY FRIEND! HE'S...."

"Well, hell, doesn't matter WHO this fly is...it's just a fuckin' fly," said Dwayne. "C'mon, the Supreme Leader's countin' on us. Let's do this." Dwayne was about to swat Buzzy off Pence's head. "Hey, where'd he go?"

Buzzy had crawled as deep as he could into Pence's hair and hung tight. He could smell Mike's fear along with that divine scalp conditioner.

"What's Trump doing?" said Zayne, looking around. "He oughta see this! It's the big moment!"

"Still gabbin' up there on the screen," answered Dwayne. "HEY, TRUMP!" He waved his arms. "IT'S HAPPENIN', MAN!"

The Supreme Leader rambled on. "The states, they want to recertify. All the Vice President needed to do was send it back to the states to recertify and we become president and you are the happiest people. But Mike didn't come through for us, even though he's sworn to uphold our beautiful Constitution. Unbelievable. He's a traitor to our great country, the best country that ever lived. He's like that famous one—Arnold. Tom Arnold, he was the biggest traitor." Jared Kushner whispered in the Supreme Leader's ear. "Benedict Arnold. Yes. Him too. Another traitor. Have you heard of him? They say he was a terrible traitor. Just like Mike. And look what happened to him. So, what are we gonna do with Traitor Mike? What do you think we should do? What should we do?"

As the crowd resumed their chant, "HANG MIKE PENCE! HANG MIKE PENCE!" the Supreme Leader grinned and moved his arms as if conducting an orchestra.

"That's right, that's right. Hang Mike Pence! It's your duty as patriots! This crowd, this crowd is unbelievable and the love I'm feeling, I've never seen anything like it, so much love.

You're very special! It's time to save our great country! We will take back our country and no one will ever take it away from me again. Believe me. I'll be your Supreme Leader forever, and never again will anyone take that away from me. Thanks to you beautiful patriots."

Pence, who had up until now remained eerily composed, began to panic as the reality of his situation sunk in. There he was, standing on a stool, now with a noose around his neck, watching the Supreme Leader's enormous orange face on the Jumbotron, ordering his faithful to actually, LITERALLY, kill him!

"ME!" thought Mike, "After all that nonsense that I took from him—the humiliation, vouching for him, covering his big fat fanny, humoring him as he pretended to be a god-fearing man when I knew darn well he was breaking the seventh commandment (with porn stars yet!) and probably the ninth one (knowing him) and I've HEARD him break number three (over and over, in fact) and I'm pretty sure he broke number eight (but did I say anything?) and hoo-boy, number one (he put himself right in the middle of that one) and now he's going to break number six, 'thou shalt not kill,' but he thinks the Lord won't notice because he's making these poor fools do the killing for him so my blood will be on THEIR hands, not his, and OH MY GOSH THEY'RE ACTUALLY GOING TO DO IT!!!"

Mike could see that Melania and Ivanka were now on the Jumbotron, smiling and waving.

"MELANIA!" screamed Pence, as loud as he could. "PLEASE! IVANKA! YOU CAN STOP THIS! Tell him this is murder! He could go to prison! Tell him what this will do to his legacy!"

Coming up close and squinting into the camera, Melania said, "I don't really care, do you?" The women threw their heads back in laughter, then poured champagne.

"We not always have been besties," said Melania to Ivanka, "but right now I'm liking you."

"I know what you mean," replied Ivanka. "Nothing brings family together like an old fashioned hanging. It's like in the good old days—more innocent times. The love just emanates from the crowd and wraps us up like we're all together in a big, warm blanket of…umm…."

"Luff?" asked Melania.

"Yes. Exactly." Ivanka smiled sweetly.

"Here's to luff!"

"And to more innocent times!"

The two women clinked glasses.

Getting restless, the mob started a new, rather awkward chant; "TELL ME WHAT DEMOCRACY LOOKS LIKE! HANGING MIKE PENCE IS WHAT DEMOCRACY LOOKS LIKE!" Due to the uneven beats in its meter, the chant quickly fell apart. Nevertheless, the Supreme Leader resumed his orchestra-conducting gestures.

Just then Mike saw Karen trying to fight her way through the angry mob toward him, but she was grabbed and held back by a pair of camo-clad brothers.

"Let me go!" she snarled at them.

"Aw, let 'er go," said another guy, close by. "It ain't her fault her husband's a traitor and a coward."

They loosened their grip, and Karen wriggled free. Upon seeing her husband propped up on the gallows, she waved her hands in the air and cried out, "Mike! Mike!"

"MOTHER!" he cried back.

"Mike, look at my nails! It's your favorite color, the one you picked out, 'Whisper Pink'!" she said, choking back tears. "You'll be OK, Honey! I'm here!"

"It's OK, Karen. I'm at peace. I'm ready. I'm ready to come home to the Lord."

"You're ready, are ya?" said Zayne. "Well all right, then! Got any last words, traitor?"

Pence closed his eyes and spoke his very last words, "Forgive them, Mother, for they know not what they do."

Zayne kicked the stool. The crowd cheered. It was over.

Buzzy's antennae were bent, both his prothorax and scutellum had been punctured, his right forewing had begun to rip away from his mesothorax, and the vision was gone in roughly half of the ommatidia in his left eye.

Bartholomew "Buzzy" Fleugon passed away on January 6th, 2021, at the exact same time as the Vice President. He died still clinging to that hair he loved so dearly.

Buzzy had packed a lot into his short life. Though it may seem short to us, at three times the average fly's lifespan, it was actually a remarkably long one. He spent his last moments on earth reflecting on what an adventurous journey it had been. He'd experienced both great joys and deep sorrows, beyond what most houseflies could even begin to imagine. He'd formed a deep and lasting bond—if only one-sided—with someone he knew in his heart to be a great man.

Word spread quickly through Washington's Cyclorrhapha community. Thousands, perhaps millions, of houseflies immediately gathered at the gallows to pay tribute to the most famous and beloved member of their species. They gingerly unfastened Buzzy's body from Pence's hair, then carried him aloft, up into the stratosphere, until his spirit jettisoned its mortal shell and floated straight to heaven. They waved their forelegs at the tiny beam of light as it passed through the pearly gates. Then they flew back down to Earth, to swarm Vice President Pence's body.

As with Buzzy, Mike's spirit cast off its physical manifestation, but instead of hurrying off to his afterlife, his spirit paused awhile, hovering over the scene below. The pandemonium he observed absolutely horrified him—the yelling, the gutteral war cries, the pounding of chests, the celebratory blasts of weapons into the air...it was deafening. On the Jumbotron, the rioters' beaming master clapped, punched his fist in the air, then gave two thumbs-up before rushing offstage and stuffing himself into a limo which whisked him off to an undisclosed location. Dwayne, Wayne, and Zayne were lifted aloft and passed around overhead through the crowd. To Mike Pence's released spirit, it resembled a mosh pit in the Seventh Circle of Hell.

"I'm ready, Lord! I can hear Gabriel's horn! Hallelujah! I'm coming home! YIPEE!!!" Mike's spirit zoomed off to Limbo, where it resides to this day, since God still can't quite decide what to do with him.

THEY GINGERLY UNFASTENED BUZZY'S BODY FROM PENCE'S HAIR, THEN CARRIED HIM ALOFT, UP INTO THE STRATOSPHERE, UNTIL HIS SPIRIT JETTISONED ITS MORTAL SHELL AND FLOATED STRAIGHT TO HEAVEN.

DREAM EIGHTEEN

HOW IT ALL ENDS
—— VERSION ONE ——

The day after the Supreme Leader lost the election, he declared himself to be "the biggest winner in history—like no one's ever seen," then immediately sealed himself and his family in the subterranean bunker below the White House and refused to leave.

Inauguration Day came and went. Having settled into the White House, President Joe and Dr. Jill Biden did their best to go about their business, but they felt uneasy knowing the former first family was below—for who knows how long?—sealed in a space with a finite supply of food and water. Even Major and Champ sensed an uneasy presence below; they kept pawing at the floor and whimpering.

The authorities set about trying to lure him out by setting traps baited with McDonald's Happy Meals just outside the bunker's entrance, while the Marine Corps Band played "Hail to the Chief." The ex-Supreme Leader did emerge, smiling and waving, but as soon as he noticed the large net about to drop on him from above, he quickly scampered back inside and slammed the door shut. He didn't come out again.

After several more botched attempts to remove the ex-Supreme Leader and his family from the bunker, a mission was launched, under the code name "Operation Wart Removal." Members of the Army Corp of Engineers, Navy Seals, Delta Force, and Orkin Pest Control, all of whom were the best in their field, made up the Tactical Extraction Team, led by

Brigadier General Beck Barley.

After many combat operation practice rounds, the team was ready. They tunneled their way to the bunker, then blasted a 12-foot hole through the 7-meter thick wall. Once the smoke cleared, the team picked their way past the rubble and entered through the supply room. There they found a disheveled ex-Supreme Leader, slumped in a corner, sucking on a rib bone.

"Sir, you and your family must come with us," said General Barley.

Wiping grease off his mouth with the end of his tie, the ex-Supreme Leader replied, "Needs salt."

"Sir, please gather your family members. We need to get going. We dynamited through the wall. This bunker could collapse any minute." General Barley looked around the empty room. "Sir? Where IS your family?"

The ex-Supreme Leader gestured toward a messy pile of bones in the corner. "I ran out of food. Nothing's left but ramen. So I had to. I was starving." Frowning, he added, "But they were too gamey." He again patted his mouth with his tie.

"Sir, you must come with us," said General Barley, more firmly this time.

"Nope. No can do. I won. The election. I won it. Bigly."

"I'm sorry to tell you, Sir, but actually, you lost. Now please come with us."

"Rigged election. So unfair. They counted all those illegal ballots."

"There were no illegal ballots, Sir. Come with us."

"The ones from shithole cities, like Detroit. And Baltimore. Those Black votes don't count. You know it. I know it."

Pointing a rib at him and squinting, he asked General Barley, "Who are you, anyway? Antifa?"

"We're a special operations unit, Sir."

"Then YOU work for ME! I command you to go away."

"Sir, you can make this easy or you can make it hard. Either way, you're coming with us."

"I order you to go get me some salt and ketchup. I'm also out of bronzer and hair spray. Then fix that hole you made, and WHAT THE HELL???" he shrieked.

General Barley had pulled out a tranquilizer gun and aimed it at the ex-Supreme Leader, who scrambled to his feet and tried to run, but the dart sunk into the meaty part of his thigh. He ran smack into a wall, then dropped like a dead walrus.

The team dragged his unconscious heft through the tunnel, then hoisted him onto a flatbed truck and secured him with bungee cords.

As the truck made its way down Pennsylvania Avenue, the street quickly filled with jubilant crowds. They sang, they danced. They threw rotten eggs and onions. "Wanna play some GOLF?" an elderly woman yelled as she threw a golf ball at him, hitting the ex-Supreme Leader squarely in the temple, momentarily waking him. "OW!" he said, rubbing his temple. He looked around. Upon seeing the cheering throngs of happy people, he smiled and waved, then murmured to himself "They love me!" before passing out again.

Soon afterward, the ex-Supreme Leader was placed under arrest, and, as a flight risk, was jailed while awaiting trial. Upon request, Lindsey Graham was allowed to join the ex-Supreme Leader in his cell, so that he could rub his feet, cut his meat up for him, apply his face bronzer, maintain his signature rococo hairstyle, and taste his food to insure it hadn't been poisoned.

Eventually the ex-Supreme Leader was prosecuted and convicted for, among other things, campaign finance violations, tax fraud, bank fraud, insurance fraud, consumer fraud, charity fraud, bribery, money laundering, obstruction of justice, pussy grabbing, inciting an insurrection, and cannibalism.

He was sentenced to fifty years in the National Zoo, where he spent most of his time hiding in his enclosure, venturing out only when visitors tossed marshmallows over the fence.

HE SPENT MOST OF HIS TIME HIDING
IN HIS ENCLOSURE, VENTURING
OUT ONLY WHEN VISITORS TOSSED
MARSHMALLOWS OVER THE FENCE.

HOW IT ALL ENDS
—VERSION TWO—

After her husband lost the election, Melania filed for divorce and returned to Slovenia to resume her "modeling" career, taking the White House silverware with her. Her last facelift left her eyes so severely squinted that she was declared legally blind. Aging, and unable to afford further plastic surgery to restore her eyesight, she sank into poverty and eventual homelessness. Known to local villagers as "Mad Mel," she roamed the streets mumbling "Be best…be best…be best…. "

Having changed his name to Barry, Barron published his memoirs about growing up the son of an orange, narcissistic father and a spooky, silent mother. Eschewing the trappings of wealth and fame, Barry lived a quiet life, tending to his organic vegetable garden, foraging for wild mushrooms, and hand-carving wooden spurtles. Through his environmental activism, he met Greta Thunberg. The two fell in love and married. Today the couple lives off the grid in a yurt in Sweden, with their many rescue animals.

Jared finally went public with his gender dysphoria. He had sexual reassignment surgery and changed her name to "Jarlene." To atone for her many misdeeds, Jarlene attended rabbinical school and became her synagogue's very first ever transgender rabbi. Jarlene and her wife Ivanka landed a reality show on TLC, "Keeping Up with the Kushners," which became a huge ratings hit.

After Junior ran a failed campaign for president with Eric as his running mate, the brothers cheered themselves up with a trip to Zimbabwe to hunt the very last living white rhino. They bribed a local Tonga guide to take them to their prey. Approaching the animal at close range from opposite sides, they both fired. They missed the rhino, but managed to shoot each other in the face, as their target trotted off into the scrub. When the guide returned to take the brothers back to the lodge, all he found was two decomposing carcasses, being picked clean by vultures. The guide was terribly distraught. He regretted not having arrived sooner, since he would have wanted to remove their heads, to be stuffed and mounted.

JARLENE ATTENDED RABBINICAL SCHOOL
AND BECAME HER SYNAGOGUE'S
FIRST EVER TRANSGENDER RABBI.

To avoid landing in prison, the ex-Supreme Leader set out to sea in a rented yacht for the island of Nogo-Nogo, which he planned to populate with his own spawn. To this end, he brought along several of his favorite blonde Fox news anchors. He also brought several dozen Happy Meals, many liters of Diet Coke, and Lindsey, as his cabin boy. The Fox blondes begged him to hire a professional ship's captain, but he said, "No one knows more about ship captaining than I do. I will be the ship-master. But you can just call me 'Master.'"

On a clear spring day, the ex-Supreme Leader took the helm, and he and his crew set sail. The yacht veered immediately off course, drifting more than 6,000 miles into the South Pacific.

One day, while rating each of the blondes on a scale of 1 to 10 on a piece of paper, the ex-Supreme Leader accidentally dropped his favorite Sharpie into the sea. Lindsey jumped off the boat to retrieve it, forgetting he couldn't swim. His body was never found.

Another tragedy occurred when the yacht capsized near a tiny island 1,500 miles east of New Zealand, and every one of the Fox blondes drowned.

However, with a body composed primarily of fat and gas, the ex-Supreme Leader was remarkably buoyant. He floated along with the tide—seabirds occasionally swooping down to peck krill from his eyebrows—and eventually washed ashore, barely conscious. A group of island dwellers pulled him out of the water and onto land.

As the island locals dragged him along the beach, his pants scooched partway down, scooping sand into his waterlogged diaper. They let go of his arms—which dropped with a wet smack—then rolled him over onto his back. A starfish clung to one side of his face. A baby octopus was tangled up in his hair.

One islander pumped his chest until out sputtered sea water, algae, and Diet Coke. The ex-Supreme Leader's eyes popped open, and he shrieked, "DON'T TOUCH ME!!!"

In spite of his belligerent demenor, his gracious and hospitable hosts tended to him until he felt better.

Once he had fully recovered, the ex-Supreme Leader took stock of his lamentable situation. 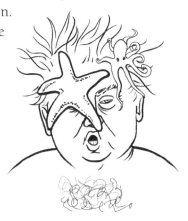 Realizing that the blondes were no longer available to him, he declared himself Supreme Leader of the island's tribe, and informed them he would take their women to be his wives. This, along with his many demands—that they bow down before him, rub his feet, and form his hair into perplexing shapes—didn't sit well with the tribe members, who had by then dubbed him "Dngi-tsbi." (Translation: "Rude and Ugly Blowfish the Color of Mango.")

So, one evening, as a red sun sank into the sea, his rescuers sacrificed the ex-Supreme Leader, along with a water buffalo. After tranquilizing the two by poison dart, they hoisted their bodies onto a wood plank placed over an open fire.

The crackles and snaps of burning fat merged with the sound of beating drums as the tribe danced around the fire, singing the sacred songs of their ancestors.

AFTER IT ALL ENDS
— OR —
DONNIE'S INFERNO

he disgraced ex-supreme leader and Melania were back at Mar-a-Lago.

"Donald you look sad. Why are you not enjoying your Happy Meal? Should make you happy, no?"

He was chewing slowly, devoid of enthusiasm. With his mouth full, he replied, "I don't get it, Malaria. I won the election. Bigly. By a landslide. It's not fair that Sleepy Joe is in the White House, and I'm here."

"Is good Donald. You now can relax. You can play with your golf. If you feel like grabbing pussy, you just do it—no one cares anymore. You no more have to pretend to like those gross people in red hats. Maybe even get your Twitter back. Going to be nice. Will be best. Trust me. Now eat more Big Mac."

He'd stopped chewing and looked down at his plate. "But, Melanie…I won."

"Eat, Donald, eat. Eat. EAT!!!"

"Huh? What's the big hurry for me to…." The ex-Supreme Leader suddenly dropped his burger. He broke out in a sweat. His face swelled up, and went from orange to red to purple to blue. He shook all over. His eyes bulged. He sputtered out "Melody, did you put something in my…ghhhhhaghhghhg…."

She smiled and said, "What? I can't understand you. Don't talk with mouth full."

"Water! Get me water," he gasped.

"Certainly darling. Do you want fizzy kind or plain?"

"PLAIN! Ghaaaaaghghgh…."

"From bottle or tap?"

"DOESN'T MATTER! Ghaghhhhghgh!!!"

"Okay, okay, I'm getting, I'm getting. Do you want with ice? Or just regular, no ice?"

"WATER! GHHHHAGHHHHGHAHG!!!!!!!!"

She casually walked over to the sink, filled a glass of water, and strode back. She held it out to his shaking hand, but just as he was about to grab it, pulled it away, saying "Whoopsies!" and laughed.

He looked at her with eyes filled with fear. "GAGHGHH???"

Melania cackled scornfully, then screamed, "YOOOOOO! How I detest you! So sick I am of your face, looks like bowl of borscht with two blobs sour cream for eyes! And your silly-shaped hair, the color of whore piss! So sick I am of you trying to put your ugly body on my nice one! You bring shame to me—everyone knows you want to make sex with your bitch daughter! You made me laughing stock! Because of you, I never will regain my career as classy porn model!"

"That's not true, Melanie," he sputtered, wheezing and clutching his chest. "The reason you can't model anymore is because you're too old and…."

She screamed, "YOU GO TO HELL!!!"

At that moment, his eyes rolled up into his head, there was a whooshing sound in his ears, and the marble floor beneath him turned to vapor. He felt a hard yank on his necktie and was pulled down, down, down by some powerful, invisible force. As he hurtled through a hot tunnel filled with acrid smoke, hissing demons flicked their pointed tongues at him and stabbed him with their tiny pitchforks as he careened past, gasping and coughing up chunks of Happy Meal, every intake

SO SICK I AM OF YOUR FACE, LOOKS
LIKE BOWL OF BORSCHT WITH
TWO BLOBS SOUR CREAM FOR EYES!

of breath like inhaling an inferno—down, down, down—until finally he landed with a thick SPLASH into a glowing river of scorching hot lava.

"WHAT THE Fffff..." he screamed, flailing around in the boiling goo.

"Here. Grab hold of the end of this oar," said a cheerful voice from behind. It belonged to a perky little demon that had sidled up next to him in a rowboat. The ex-Supreme Leader grabbed the oar, and the demon, who was apparently incredibly strong for his diminutive size, pulled him in close, then helped hoist him into the boat.

"Where the hell AM I???"

The demon smiled warmly and replied, "Yes! Welcome to Hell! Well, almost, anyway... we'll be there in a few. My name is Fenriz. Pleased to meet you. Sorry 'bout the circumstances."

"Jesus fucking Chr..."

"Uh-oh. You just took His name in vain," said Fenriz, who stopped rowing long enough to jot something down on a notepad. "That will add another ten years to your eternal stay here."

"There's been a mistake. Didn't you see that picture of me holding a Bible? Christians are crazy about me. Everyone knows it."

"Actually, those particular 'Christians' quit following the good Lord's teachings, and started worshipping you, their very own golden calf (or, in your case, corpulent bovine). And you loved it! Tsk tsk!" said Fenriz, wagging a skinny red index finger back and forth. "Not that I care. Just sayin'," he shrugged.

Soon the boat bumped up against the iron gates of Hell.

"Here's your stop, chief. Go through the gates. Your chaperone is waiting on the other side. Ciao!"

HIS EYES ROLLED UP INTO HIS HEAD, THERE
WAS A WHOOSHING SOUND IN HIS EARS,
AND THE MARBLE FLOOR BENEATH HIM
TURNED TO VAPOR. HE FELT A HARD YANK
ON HIS NECKTIE AND WAS PULLED
DOWN, DOWN, DOWN...

"Wait! What time are you picking me up to take me back? I haven't even finished my hamberder."

"Oh, at about...." he squinted down at his wrist. "Never. Hee hee! Have a good afterlife!"

As the tiny demon rowed away, the iron gates of Hell swung open, with a loud groaning sound. The dead Supreme Leader passed through. The air was thick with sulfur and hellfire. A very large demon with huge wings greeted him.

"Welcome to Hades, my friend! Or should I say 'my fiend'? My name is Jinxonicus Sixtus, but my fiends just call me Jinx. Please step this way."

Walking on all fours, Jinxonicus led the dead Supreme Leader down a nondescript corridor and into a room that looked very much like the Department of Motor Vehicles. Jinx instructed him to take a seat, and handed him a pen and clipboard. "We need you to fill out these intake forms. There are 666,666,666 pages, but no worries—there's plenty of time. Eternity, in fact! HA! Ahhh....That never gets old."

"Where's Lindsey? Lindsey can do this for me."

"Sorry, chief—I don't know any Lindseys down here. You're on your own."

Furious, the dead Supreme Leader said, "I'm not filling these out! I'm Donald Trump, Supreme Leader of the United States, super-successful real estate titan, bestselling author, host of the "The Apprentice," which, by the way, had YUGE ratings when I was host, but then Schwarzeneg...."

"Oh, my—please forgive me!" interrupted Jinx. "I didn't recognize you with your hair singed off. We've been expecting you! The forms can wait. Let me escort you to our VIP lounge. You can have a welcome cocktail and hobnob with some other celebrity A-list guests."

On their way to the VIP lounge, they were flanked by throngs of sobbing, screaming, moaning, tormented souls.

The dead Supreme Leader asked Jinx, "Who are these losers? Muslims? Illegals? Socialists?"

"In life they were the big money donors to your campaigns. Rich, but not famous enough to have gained VIP status, which is the ultimate eternal torture for them. They tend to gather outside the lounge, still hoping to get in. Here you go."

They entered a spacious lounge. VIPs were sitting at the tiki-themed bar, sipping flaming cocktails and munching raw habanero peppers from snack bowls. "How Am I Supposed to Live Without You" was playing in the background, on repeat.

"Here. You get five free drink tickets. If you want extras, let me know; you can earn more by sucking on my balls. See ya later, instigator!"

"Good to know, good to know," replied the dead Supreme Leader, giving a thumbs-up. He plopped down on a barstool.

"What'll ya have?" asked the bartender, Jim Jones. "Today's cocktail special is Absinthe Toddy."

"Diet Coke," replied the dead Supreme Leader. Jones filled a goblet with boiling hot Coca-Cola and handed it to him.

Scanning the room, the dead Supreme Leader thought to himself, "Wow—this really IS the big league!" It was a virtual "Who's Who" of some of history's most notorious sinners. There was Saddam Hussein, Joseph Stalin, Charles Manson, Idi Amin, Pol Pot, Kim Jong-il, Warren Jeffs, Roger Ailes, Vlad the Impaler....

"SHELDON!!!" shouted the dead Supreme Leader, upon seeing his old pal, sitting alone. "What a surprise! Great to see you! What are you doing down here? I thought you'd have gone the other direction," he said, pointing upward. "At least you made VIP status! I'm a little surprised, quite frankly. Bartender, get Mr. Adelson a Manischewitz."

"Donald?! When did YOU get here?" asked Sheldon Adelson.

"Just now!"

"My goodness, what happened?"

"I was rescuing these kids from an orphanage that had been set on fire by Antifa, when...."

Sheldon interrupted. "Come now, Donald—don't give me any of your shmegeggy."

"I think Melania poisoned me."

"Oy gevalt!" Sheldon shook his head. "But I'm sorry to say I'm not so surprised. Donald, I say this with love...I never trusted that shiksa whore. Her eyes, they remind me of the slots in my casinos. When I look at her, I half expect to hear 'bing bing bing bing!'" He swirled his wine, sniffed it, took a sip. "Mmm... complex yet well balanced, with hints of Welch's grape jelly."

Gesturing around the room, Sheldon continued. "Can you believe this? What IS this mishegas? We end up in hell? After all the good we did? I guess they mistook us for a couple of shmendricks. Oy, it's hot down here. I'm schvitzing!"

"Where's Epstein? You know Jeffrey's gotta be here. He can hook us up with some girls. Betcha there's some hot numbers around here, am I right?"

Adelson moaned, "It's torture! All these gorgeous demon ladies running around half naked with their big pointy boobies and nice round tuchuses, and can you believe it? My schmeckel doesn't work! It's like a tired old floppy herring." He added, sadly, "This is how they punish us. Yours won't work either."

"Oh, it will, believe me, believe me," the dead Supreme Leader winked. "You'll see."

"I'd rather not."

"Now, where in hell are all these sexy ladies hiding?"

"I'm right here!" Anita Bryant called out from the end of the bar. She was dressed in a black latex catsuit with holes cut out at the breasts and crotch. Holding up her flaming Screwdriver, she added, "Cheers!" The little umbrella in her drink suddenly caught fire. She stuck it in her mouth to put out the flame, making a hissing sound. Steam puffed out her ears and nostrils.

MEANWHILE, back on earth....

It's a crisp, sunny Friday the 13th. Rudy Giuliani is whistling on his way from the parking garage to the courthouse for his trial. Ignoring the caution signs on a sidewalk abutting a construction site, he passes under a ladder. Suddenly, a black cat crosses his path. Tripping over the cat, Rudy lands on a banana peel, slips, cracks his head open, spilling his brains all over the sidewalk, and the next moment....

"RUDY!!! What are you doing here?" asked a surprised dead Supreme Leader.

Brushing cinders off his lapels, Rudy said, "Jesus Christ! Where am I? Am I dead? Jeez. I guess I shouldn't have walked under that ladder, dammit."

"Look on the bright side," said the dead Supreme Leader. "You won't have to go to prison. And we can hang out together! For eternity!"

"Eternity. Oy. Why am I here?" whined Sheldon, rubbing his temples. "After all my philanthropic work I belong in Heaven, with the mensches. That was the whole point, after all."

"Sheldon, are you kidding me? You'd rather be in Heaven, with all those losers? Sitting on a cloud, listening to Eleanor Roosevelt play harp all damn day? Everyone flitting around in white robes? Enya music? FOR ETERNITY? Boring!!! Anyway, it doesn't seem so bad down here for us VIPs. Jinx was telling me that besides this lounge, there's a sinema, an all-you-can-eat buffet, even a golf course!"

"You just got here, Donald," Sheldon replied. "Little do you know. The golf course? Those sand traps are quicksand. If you get stuck in one, that's where you'll spend eternity, up to your ass in muck, tossing Hitler's balls back to him."

Just then Jinx reappeared, escorting a dazed, trembling man into the lounge.

"LINDSEY?! No—you, too?" said the dead Supreme Leader.

Lindsey Graham had two black eyes, a split lip, and purple bruises all over his body.

"I'm dead? Shoot," said a shaken Graham.

"What the hell happened to you? You look awful!" asked the dead Supreme Leader.

"I went to a Proud Boys meeting, thinkin' it was something entirely different than what it turned out to be. Trust me— those aren't no 'boys'! They're big scary men with beards and stuff. When I tried to leave they were on me like cheese on a cracker, hittin' me, and calling me 'traitor' and 'little bitch'.... Oh lord!" He gently patted his swollen lip with his fingertips.

"It's all good now, Linno," the dead Supreme Leader reassured him. "You're safe. Jinx here, he's a big strong guy, very strong, very tough—he'll take good care of you, won't you, Jinx? Jinxy, show Mr. Graham the intake room so he can start filling out those forms for me. And go get me another Coke."

Jinxonicus Sixtus suddenly reared up on his hind legs. Seeming to quadruple in size, he stretched his enormous wings to their full width, and bellowed, "YOU do not give the orders here—I DO! As a proxy for Lucifer, deputized by the Devil himself, I CONDEMN YOU TO ETERNAL PUNISHMENT!

"YOU ARE NOBODY!!!"

"Wrong!" said the dead Supreme Leader. Turning to his friends, he added, "So nasty."

The mighty gust of breath that Jinxonicus blasted the dead Supreme Leader's way was so ghastly in its stench—such a vile, noxious mix of fetid swamp water, toe fungus, hot cabbage farts, rotting durian, sweaty feet, rancid ham, gangrenous flesh, decomposing bullfrog, pus oozing from a grizzly bear's infected anal sac, and the morning breath of a hundred frat boys after a long night of consuming beer and bad clams, then vomiting it all up and forgetting to brush their teeth—that it knocked the dead Supreme Leader off his feet.

"Uh oh," whispered Graham, nervously patting his lip. "He looks pissed."

"Donald J. Trump, I hereby charge you with having committed all seven deadly sins, over and over and over again!"

"Fake news," yawned the dead Supreme Leader.

"QUIET!!!" Jinx boomed. "You shall receive the following punishments, in seven consecutive sentences."

Fenriz popped up, clutching a stack of seven cue cards.

THE PUNISHMENTS

He danced a little jig, then held up a card that read **PRIDE**.

Jinxonicus solemnly pronounced, "You will be stripped of all your clothing except for your fully-loaded diaper and your necktie, which I will use as a leash for parading you past the jeering sinners who had supported you in life. Your few remaining strands of hair will be pulled straight up and worn in a ponytail on top of your head, tied in a little pink bow."

Fenriz spun around once, then held up another card that read **GREED**.

Waving a cloven hoof toward an enormous mountain of coins in the distance, Jinxonicus asked, "Do you see that pile of change? You will count every single nickel, dime, and penny, and insert them into paper coin tubes. You will then bring them to our accounting office and report the total sum.

Our accountants will add them up. If your count is off by even one cent, you will receive severe lashings by our demons from the IRS, who are particularly upset with you and eager for retribution. You will then begin the process all over again, until you get it right."

Fenriz did a quick moonwalk, then held up **LUST**.

Jinx continued, "You will perform fellatio on a maggot-infested kielbasa while simultaneously being sodomized by conjoined twin proboscis monkeys with genital warts. This disturbing (yet fascinating!) spectacle will take place before a large audience, which should actually please you, since you love nothing more than to hold a big crowd in your thrall. After the live show, all will be invited to the sinema for popcorn and a screening (at long last!) of the pee tape."

Here Fenriz did a step-shuffle-step, then held up **ENVY**.

Said Jinx, "Strapped into a chair with metal clamps holding your eyelids open, you will watch a montage on an endless loop of Barack Obama's best speeches, including the one before his enormous and adoring inauguration crowd. Not only will you be forced to endure his deft comic timing, effortless charm, keen intelligence, and undeniable charisma, you'll also be treated to split-screen shots comparing his physique with your own."

Fenriz jumped up and landed in a split ("He's good," whispered Lindsey) then held up **GLUTTONY**.

Jinx continued, "You will be frozen up to your sternum in a vat of mint chip ice cream which will be topped with a layer of burning hot fudge, as demons jab you with ice cream spoons and pelt you with piping hot nuts."

After doing a somersault, Fenriz held up **WRATH**.

Said Jinx, "I seem to recall you made a campaign promise to bring back waterboarding, and, I quote, '…a hell of a lot worse.' But once you were in office, your advisors didn't allow it. I can only imagine how terribly disappointing that must have been for you." He pouted while wiping an imaginary tear from his cheek, then grinned.

"Well, you inspired us! Your dream of waterboarding will finally be fulfilled, right here in Hades! And YOU, my friend, will be our very first guest to be waterboarded!" Fenriz dropped his cards to clap excitedly and jump up and down.

"But our version has been customized just for you!" Jinx continued. "Instead of water, you will be treated to a steady dribble of cold pee."

Fenriz held up the last cue card: **SLOTH**.

Said Jinx, "It's about time you did an honest day's work. Therefore I sentence you to mop the floors of every single one of the underworld's lavatories. With your tongue.

"Once you have completed all seven sentences, you will appear before Lucifer. If you have performed your punishments to his satisfaction, you can return to the VIP lounge, where you will be treated to more of Michael Bolton's greatest hits. But only after you've finished filling out those intake forms, with a very, very, VERY dry felt-tip marker.

"Now, LET THE PUNISHMENTS BEGIN!!!"

With that, Fenriz blasted a loud, squawky note on a trumpet, then dropped to one knee and made a final florid rolling gesture of his arm.

The next time Sheldon, Rudy, and Lindsey saw their old fiend, Jinxonicus Sixtus was walking him on his leash to Lucifer's chamber, past crowds of jeering, cackling, howling, tortured souls.

* WELL, NOT REALLY.
AFTER ALL, ETERNITY HAS NO END.

HAIKU BY THE SUPREME LEADER

Did you know that the Supreme Leader is a renowned master of the art of haiku? When he is in a reflective mood, he likes to contemplate the beauty of the natural world, and ponder the intricacies of life. Here are some examples of his best poems.

Ivanka is hot
Junior looks a lot like me
Should have stopped at two.

The election was
stolen by that Sleepy Joe
I won it, bigly.

I like hamberders
no lettuce, just a slice of
American cheese.

Kellyanne looks strange
her two eyeballs do not match
one is higher up.

Sleepy Joe will ban
candy, gum, and ice cream too
all that we hold dear.

Poor Melania
isn't a ten anymore.
Time for a new wife.

No collusion! It's
just Fake News made up by the
failing New York Times.

My haikus are best
They are really tremendous
Everyone's saying.

Madame Pelosi
or as I call her, "Nancy"
she's not very nice.

The best taco bowls
are made in Trump Tower Grill
I love Hispanics!

A HOLIDAY LETTER
FROM
MELANIA

From the Desk of Melania K. Trump

January 1st, 2022

Greetings! Is me, Melania, with End-of-Year Xmas Holiday Letter! (I know, I know, little late, so sue me...I sue you right back, haha.)

I hope you had Happy Xmas! I say "Xmas," never "holiday," because of terrible war on Xmas. I say "Happy Xmas" no matter what is holiday; I say for Easter, Valentine's...also birthdays. I'm on side of Xmas, always.

War against Xmas is such terrible thing, reminds me of Slovenian Independence War of 1991...I was young girl just starting out career as porn model when war happened, making for difficult start for me. But I pulled through and was great success as model anyways. So proud of Donald I am, for being first president ever to end war on Xmas. Is one of many big accomplishments as U.S. President!

Why does not everybody love Xmas, I don't understand. Especially Jewish people, since Christ was Jew himself, why they not celebrate his birthday? Besides, Xmas is so much more nice than boring Hanukkah. What's with menorah? Is just candleholder! And only eight presents per Jew? Are you kidding me? And stupid dreidel...it spins, so what? If we gave Barron dreidel for Xmas when little boy, he would have thrown it out window.

Sanny Claus always brings Barron many classy presents, like Trump cologne, Trump golf balls, Trump National Hotel towel and laundry bag....

Let's face it—real reason for war on Xmas is because of Jewish people being SO jealous of our presents and our Sanny Claus and his flying deer and our nice songs like "Be Best Ye Merry Gentlemen," and "All I Want for Xmas Is 18 Karat Gold Van Cleef Bracelet and You."

I tell you secret. Xmas for me was not always like is now. When I was little girl in Slovenia we had different customs. We not have Sanny Claus, can you believe it? We have instead Gospa Ula, old lady with one eye, like Cyclops. Each Xmas Eve, Ula would mount huge grizzly bear and ride bear to every village in Slovenia, stopping at each house, then make bear wait while she break window, climb inside, and pour ladle of hot cabbage soup into rubber galoshes we left near fireplace.

Next day, everyone has to get windows repaired and throw out ruined galoshes.

Is why I dreamed of leaving Slovenia, marry rich American guy and have proper Xmas, nice gifts. Rest is history.

Anyway, reason for this letter is telling you of year we had. It start out exciting, with brave patriots breaking into ugly old capitol building to kill Mike Pence and give White House back to Trump family. I not even like White House, but is rightfully ours. Sadly, day not went according to plan. What you can do but roll with punches? Is not so easy for Donald—every single day is "traitor Mike this" and "Cheney bitch that"—I tell him hush, go play some golf, but Donald still fuming.

Me? I move on, no problem.

Since I no more am First Lady I have time finally for other stuffs. No more have to go visit dirty children at border, or ruin good Blahnik pumps sloshing around Texas hurricane.

And so—very excited I am today to announce my brand new project; BUY MELANIA'S STUFFS!!! What is? I tell you!

You can buy my pictures as thing called NFT. What NFT is is some kind of not-fun token. I don't really understand, except means you can be proud owner of painting of my beautiful eyes for only hundred fifty dollars. You own painting but not actually *have* it, so no need to store or keep in vault because is not really there, but still you get to brag to friends you are owner of my eyeballs.

Also, you can buy token painting of me in white hat I wore to visit French President and his short dumpy wife.

And another more thing; you even can buy my real actual hat! Is in auction, starting bid $250,000. Be very valuable one day. Also in auction—my famous I Really Don't Care jacket, my Christian Louboutin shoes, my nighty, my pantyhose, my undies, my spanx…so much more!

Just go to BuyMelaniaStuffs.com to make bid, right now. A portion of monies from sales will go to unfortunate foster care children, to help them be best. (How much portion? Who knows?) Help get them on own two feet after too old for foster system. Maybe train girls to be sexy models like me. Or boys to work for Donald. I don't know. We'll see.

What else, what else….Can't think.

Ok is good for now, bye.

WHAT NFT IS IS SOME KIND OF
NOT-FUN TOKEN.
I DON'T REALLY UNDERSTAND, EXCEPT
MEANS YOU CAN BE PROUD OWNER
OF PAINTING OF MY BEAUTIFUL EYES
FOR ONLY 150 DOLLARS.
YOU OWN IT BUT NOT ACTUALLY HAVE IT,
SO NO NEED TO STORE OR KEEP IN VAULT,
BECAUSE IS NOT REALLY THERE,
BUT STILL YOU GET TO BRAG TO FRIENDS
YOU ARE OWNER OF MY EYEBALLS.

NOTES

Cover: *Christ in Limbo* is by a follower of Hieronymus Bosch, Netherlandish, 1450–1516. It's been altered by me.

Pages 121–125: The illustration of the demon "Yan-gant-y-tan" is by Louis Le Breton, and then engraved as woodcuts by M. Jarrault, for *Dictionnaire Infernal,* which first appeared in 1818, Yup, it's been altered by me.

Page 126: I could not find any information on this painting (which I'd altered, of course) other than that it's a depiction of Naraka, which is a term in Buddhist cosmology similar to the Christian Hell or purgatory. Burmese representation, 19th c.

Page 128–129: *The Pine Trees* by Hasegawa Tohaku, late 16th century.

Page 129: The very last haiku is taken verbatim from Trump's tweet. (!!!)

Page 132: Melania actually does have a website from which she sells NFTs of a painting of her eyes, and auctioned off the white hat she wore to meet the Macrons. I did not make that up.

The font used for the title and initial caps is Pandemica Bold, which I created for this book.

This is a work of fiction.
Though many of the characters named are actual
public figures, and some of what takes place was inspired
by real events, these stories are completely, utterly, absolutely,
indisputably, thoroughly, entirely, clearly, OBVIOUSLY
made up (except where direct quotes are noted).

aruška Lipski has long felt she is a writer trapped inside the body of a graphic designer. As an illustrator, her work appeared in various national publications. In the 1980s and '90s, Lipski was a performance artist, in collaboration with Tom Koken, whose character "Frieda" was a popular cult figure in NYC's club scene. She also performed as "Frieda" at Wigstock festivals, in various art spaces, at the Institute of Contemporary Arts in London, and on "Late Night with David Letterman." Videos starring "Frieda"—made in collaboration with Koken and Tom Rubnitz—have been shown in art museums worldwide. As the offspring of Conservative Republican parents, Baruška voted for Nixon in her junior high school's mock election, but by Nixon's second term she had become a full-fledged lefty. Thanks to the inspiration sparked by both Donald Trump and the Arc of the Viral Universe project, Baruška has at last liberated her inner wordsmith.

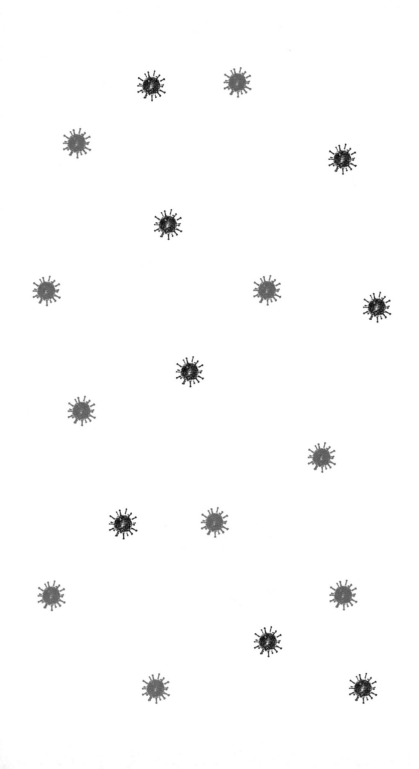

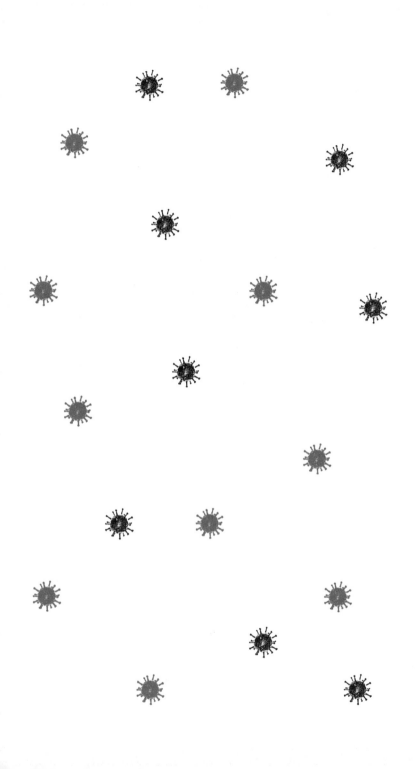

Made in the USA
Columbia, SC
14 August 2022

64529179R10078